I'D BEEN ~~TRICKED...~~

What felt like about forty NFL linebackers jumped astraddle me and started trying to beat what little brains I got to a pulp. My ears were ringing and I thought, "I'm gonna die on a residential street in Houston, Texas." It was a sad thought, indeed.

Then I started hearing things other than the beating of my own blood. A high whining sound, the crunch of metal on metal, a screech, a yell, a yip of pain, then saw four pairs of feet running by me and heard a voice sounding a lot like Chuck's.

I looked up to see my baby sister's children gathered around me, Leonard with a fireplace tool in his hand, the end of it shiny from something wet that I hoped was one of my assailants' blood, Carl standing there with his little league baseball bat, and Marlene with a spray bottle of ammonia.

"We got 'em. You see that, Uncle Chuck?"

———————— ★ ————————

HOUSTON IN THE REARVIEW MIRROR

SUSAN ROGERS COOPER

WORLDWIDE®

TORONTO • NEW YORK • LONDON
AMSTERDAM • PARIS • SYDNEY • HAMBURG
STOCKHOLM • ATHENS • TOKYO • MILAN
MADRID • WARSAW • BUDAPEST • AUCKLAND

HOUSTON IN THE REARVIEW MIRROR

A Worldwide Mystery/May 1992

First published by St. Martin's Press Incorporated.

ISBN 0-373-26095-4

To Don and Evin, always,
and
To Kathy,
for her faith, support, and truth,
lo these many years.

ONE

WHO WAS IT that said, "Some days are diamonds, some days are stone"? John Denver? Doesn't matter; I got another line to add to it, though. "Some days are pure and simple dog shit." Might not rhyme, but it's apt. That's the kind of day it was. That Friday in mid-February with the wind wailing in from the north, colder than a witches tit. Nothing between me and Canada but a barbed-wire fence, as my Daddy used to say.

Some days the minute you get out of bed you know what kind of day it's gonna be. The minute I got out of bed that Friday, I stubbed my toe on the bedside table so hard I nearly broke it. That was just about the best part of the day.

My name's Milton Kovak. I'm chief deputy for the Prophesy County, Oklahoma, Sheriff's Department. It's not a bad job. I get to drive a county car and they gave me my own gun. But sometimes the job can get on your nerves. Like that Friday.

I walked into my office at the Sheriff's Department that morning and got a call first thing that JoBeth McKenzie was beating up on her kid again.

So I went over. This time she'd broken his arm. What do you do? I'd turned her over to the County Welfare people fifteen times, and that's in the record books, but they keep giving her back the little boy. So I got into a fight with the officious little lady who called herself a social worker and said a few things I shouldn't have said, I guess. At least that's what the sheriff said when he called me on the carpet about it. He admitted he agreed with everything I'd said but still felt I shouldn't have said it. Explain that one to me.

So then I had to take a prisoner over to Shanks County, which is over one hundred miles away, and I had to take Mike Neils with me. Mike is one of the deputies. One of the most irritating people you're ever likely to meet. He's like a puppy that pees on your leg a lot. And I had to listen to him the whole way back and if there's one thing Mike Neils is plenty capable of doing it's talking nonstop for one hundred miles.

And the day just went on in that vein. So that when I got home to my new house on Mountain Falls Road, where the only living things to greet me were my plant and my cat, Evinrude, I was still barely calmed down, even though the eighteen-mile trip from the station to my house usually did a lot toward steadying my nerves.

Let me tell you about my house. It's a great house. My ex-wife called it a crazy house and had refused to buy it when we'd first looked at it more than eight years ago. But then, after the divorce, for reasons I'm not about to go into, the house went on the market again. And I bought it. It's a nine-room house and I got about one and a half rooms of furniture. The lack of furniture makes the place look smaller for some perverse reason. One of these days I'm gonna do something about that. The lack of furniture, I mean. I been trying to talk Glenda Sue Robertson, my lady friend, into helping me decorate but to her that means some kind of commitment she's not willing to make.

So anyway, I was sitting home that evening in my windowed room with my first light beer of the day and thinking about the fact that Glenda Sue Robertson and I had made love in almost every room of this house. In the bedroom, which was only right, once in the shower, couple of times in front of the fireplace in the living room, at night on the deck in a broken-down lounge chair, and once even standing up in the kitchen after we'd both had a few. But we'd never made love in my used-to-be-favorite room of the house, the windowed room on the second floor. And, of course, I knew why. I knew why Glenda Sue had never even been in the windowed room. Because that was where the former lady of the house and I had spent many a cozy evening naked under an afghan. Her name was Laura. The former lady of the house. Laura Johnson. And because of her, I was treating Glenda Sue Robertson, one of the nicest ladies I've ever known, like a red-headed stepchild. I decided that when Glenda Sue came over that night, I was gonna show her the windowed room. And anything else she wanted to see. (That's a joke.)

So she got there, Glenda Sue did, and I fixed us both a couple of beers and took her up the stairs to the windowed room and showed her the great view. She was impressed and she didn't say a word about never having seen the room before and why was that, which I figured was nice of her, but like I said, Glenda Sue's a nice lady. And things happen the way things do and before we knew it, Glenda Sue and I were on the floor. And then something happened that had never happened to me before except once when I was drunker than I ought to have been. Or rather, something didn't happen, if you know what I mean. And Glenda Sue was real nice about it. Of course, women are always real nice about *that* to your face. God only knows, though, what they tell their girlfriends. And I just laid there and cursed Laura Johnson silently to myself.

So that's when Glenda Sue got the bright idea to move the scene of the crime, so to speak, and we headed downstairs to the master bedroom where, lo and behold . . .

And then the phone rang.

And as I wasn't on call, I just said, "Hello?"

And the male voice said, "Milton Kovak, please."

"That's me."

"Are you the Milton Kovak whose sister is Jewel Kovak Hotchkiss?"

And that's when there was a repeat of my little disaster in the windowed room.

"Yeah. She's my sister. Who's this?"

"Mr. Kovak, I'm sorry to have to tell you this. My name's Lincoln. David Lincoln. Sergeant David Lincoln with the Houston Police Department? Sir, your sister is in critical condition at Ben Taub Hospital here in Houston . . ."

"Oh, my God!"

"And her husband, Henry Hotchkiss?"

"Yeah?"

"Well, he's dead, sir."

"Oh, shit. Oh, Jesus. What was it? A car wreck?"

"Well, no, sir—It appears, Mr. Kovak, like it was a murder-suicide. Except your sister didn't aim so straight when she held the gun to her head."

Now, you just try having someone call you up in the middle of the night and tell you something like that. No, don't. Don't try that. It doesn't feel at all good.

"Where are the kids?"

"They were all at a high school basketball game when it happened. They were the ones who found them and called it in."

"Oh, sweet Jesus. How's Jewel? How bad is it?"

"She's in a coma, Mr. Kovak." We were both silent for a minute and I thanked the Lord that I was lucky enough to get me a sensitive cop calling. As a cop myself, I know how these things are sometimes handled, which isn't good at all. For some strange reason I remembered the time, about three weeks after Mike Neils joined the force, when he had to do what Lincoln was doing. He came back to the station with the imprint of a hot iron on the side of his face. Seemed the lady he was trying to tell about her husband's fatal car wreck on the interstate just wasn't having any of it.

Probably Mr. Lincoln, David, Sergeant, was lucky he was doing his job over the phone. But he was okay, as far as death messengers went. "Mr.

Kovak? The kids have been taken to a shelter for the night. I was hoping you could get down here…"

"Yeah. I'm on my way. What's your number?" I wrote the information down on the receipt for some cough drops I'd bought a month ago that still sat on my bedside table. When we hung up, I lay down next to Glenda Sue and stared at the ceiling. After a while, I could tell her what happened.

Well, I suppose Glenda Sue's had enough grief in her life where she knows how to deal with it. Because deal with it is what she did. After holding me for a minute, she got up, got dressed, got on the phone and made me reservations for a flight from Tulsa to Houston, and then set about gathering up my dirty clothes to wash so I'd have something to wear. I suppose I wouldn't have thought of that.

I guess you could say I've known Glenda Sue Robertson all my life, practically. Since the first grade, anyway, for sure. She was Glenda Sue Davies then. In grade school, her, me, and Lin Robertson were like the three musketeers. Me and Lin forgave Glenda Sue for being a girl and the three of us did just about everything together. It wasn't until high school, when Glenda Sue got knockers, that Lin and I noticed that she was of the female persuasion. That's when Lin and her became an item. You couldn't blame Glenda Sue. He was a bigger stud football player than me. Those things mattered back then. But that was okay, because right after they got together is when I met my then future and now ex-wife.

When we graduated, I went smack into the Air Force and Lin and Glenda Sue got smack pregnant. Actually, Glenda Sue was the one with the swelled-up belly. They got married as fast as possible, which is what you did in those days in such a situation. Six months later their daughter, Melissa, was born and that's when Lin started showing just how stupid he was.

Most of what I know about their early days I got secondhand, but at some point shortly after their daughter's birth, Lin found himself a new hobby, namely getting drunk and beating up on Glenda Sue. Knowing her like I do now, I don't really understand why she put up with it. It wasn't like he was supporting her financially or anything. Glenda Sue made all the money in that family with her waitressing job. Maybe it was a mothering thing, I don't know. But she stayed with him, up until Melissa reached puberty and Lin got the bright idea to start messing with her. That's when Glenda Sue sent him to the hospital with a concussion from a well-wielded baseball bat.

I'd been with the Department for a while by then and had been pulled into the fracas many a time when little Melissa would come running to us to take her daddy off her mama. Couple of times I tried talking to Lin about it. When he was sober he'd say things like ''I know, I know. It's terrible. It's the booze, Milt. Just the booze, I swear to God. And I'll never touch another drop.'' The next night, he'd get drunk again and do it all over again. The one time I tried to talk to him when he was drunk he took a swing at me.

By the time Glenda Sue finally came after him with the baseball bat, the marriage was over, basically, though Lin did keep trying to come home from time to time. Although all he got for it was a butt full of buckshot from his own shotgun. He finally wandered out of the county for good.

Like I said, I'd known Glenda Sue all my life and right after my wife divorced me, I ended up in bed with my old friend, but all it did was make me feel dog-shit awful. So instead of sticking with something known like Glenda Sue, I ended up making a jackass out of myself over a married lady named Laura Johnson. The one who lived in my house before I bought it. After she left town, with me feeling about as low as I could possibly get, I found myself dead drunk over at the Longbranch Inn one evening. Glenda Sue took me home and washed my face and sobered me up and told me if I ever got drunk around her again she'd put Ipecac in my beer. We've been seeing each other on at least a weekly basis ever since.

Glenda Sue Robertson knew her business. By five A.M. Saturday morning, we were on our way to Tulsa. The flight left at seven-thirty and I'd just about make it there on time. We were silent most of the way, what talking we did having to do with things other than my sister.

Finally, after figuring out which terminal and which parking lot we needed, we managed to make it inside and to my gate.

Waiting for my flight, Glenda Sue kissed me and held me for a minute.

"Milton, you need anything, you holler, okay?"

"Yeah. Thanks, Glenda Sue."

"I mean it. Meanwhile, you take as long as you need. I'll water your plant and feed Evinrude. You don't worry about that."

"Shit. I forgot to call the sheriff."

We looked around for a pay phone. I still had twenty minutes before my flight. I called Elberry Blankenship, Sheriff of Prophesy County and my boss.

"Goddam, Milton, you know what time it is?"

"Sorry, Elberry . . . I got bad news."

He woke up fast. "What is it?"

So I told him.

He sighed long and heavy. "Jesus, boy, I'm sorry. I really, truly am. Little Jewel. Shit. That's just not worth believing."

"I'm in Tulsa now, Elberry, plane leaves in just a few minutes. . . ."

"Take all the time you need, Milt. Don't worry about us."

"Thanks, Sheriff."

"And, Milt, you need anything . . ."

"Yes, sir, thank you."

And we hung up. When they called the flight, Glenda Sue kissed me again and I got on the plane.

Now, strangely enough, for having spent three years in the Air Force, I hate flying. I mean, I *hate* it. I'd rather dip my naked body in melted Crisco than get up in one of those contraptions. But there are times when a man's got to do and all that dog shit. And this was one of those times. So I talked the little girl with the false eyelashes who was trying to serve me breakfast into serving me drinks instead.

Now, for a couple of hours in the air a body can think about things like how in the hell an airplane stays up, or how far down the ground is, or if this is the pilot's first solo flight, or any number of negative things. Or a body can get drunk and let his thoughts sorta roam around. Which is what I decided to do. And for the first time since her death, I truly missed Mama. I could have used a little of that lady's gumption right about then.

I remember a story Daddy used to tell about Mama every chance he got. It was about their courting days. Being a country boy, my daddy had country-boy habits, one of which was spitting. He didn't chew tobacco or anything (actually he smoked three packs of Lucky Strikes a day till the day he died—of a heart attack), he just would spit. Anywhere, any time. Hock him up a good one, he used to say. Well, Mama and Daddy started seeing each other when she was fifteen and he was nineteen and she bitched from day one about his spitting. She'd say, according to Daddy, "Herbert, that's the nastiest habit a body can have. If you don't stop it, I won't go out with you no more."

Well, Daddy being Daddy, or any well brought up country boy, he wasn't about to let some fifteen-year-old girl tell him what to do. So she'd break up with him for a week or so than start seeing him again, and nagging all over again. Finally, after they'd been seeing each other for about a year, Mama stopped nagging. Daddy said he figured he'd finally gotten his way. Until they were walking up the sidewalk toward the church one Sunday morning and Daddy spat upon the sidewalk, whereupon Mama hocked her up a good one and aimed it right on top of Daddy's head. Daddy stopped in his tracks, looked around at the people going into the church and said, "Girl, you got me." And he never spit again.

I remember a time I personally saw my mama in action. And it was the damnedest thing. We had this family living next door to us in this rented house. The husband was a long-distance trucker who, I suppose, had a thing about never leaving his woman alone unpregnant. They had ten kids, and when they moved in next door to us, four of the ten were still in diapers: two-year-old twin boys, a girl a little over a year old, and a new baby.

Mama decided to call on the lady like neighbors did in those days, bringing over some homemade cobbler (one of the few things my mama could cook that didn't kill anybody outright). I was about ten years old at the time and Mama took me with her on her call, figuring one of the kids had to be about my age.

The lady, I remember her name was Mrs. Barker, answered the door with the one-year-old on her hip and the twins hanging on to either leg. More kids were screaming and running around the living room. The most kids I'd ever seen outside of a classroom. She was real nice and invited us in and we followed her to the kitchen where she deposited the cobbler.

"My husband's coming home tonight," she announced.

Mama smiled and said, "Well, that's good. I know you must miss him."

"Oh, yes," she said, smiling. "I fixed him a special meal. It's in the oven now."

That's when I heard the baby crying. And so did Mama.

"Where's that new baby of yours?" Mama asked.

"Why, right here," Mrs. Barker had answered, indicating the one-year-old on her hip. Again we heard the cry of a baby.

I was getting scared. Really scared. But Mama looked as calm as anything when she said, "So what you fixing your man for dinner?"

Again Mrs. Barker beamed. "A roast."

"Um, well, it sure smells good. Mind if a take a look?"

She grabbed up a dish rag and went to the oven and pulled it open. There in a big pot covered with carrots and potatoes was the new little baby.

Mama picked the baby up and handed it to me and pushed me toward the back door. "Mrs. Barker," she said, "I think you got the wrong roast in here. Let me take this one away and I'll get you a good roast beef. How does that sound?"

"Where's that boy going with my dinner?" Mrs. Barker asked, but I was already out the door and headed to the back door of our house.

The upshot of the whole thing was that Mama called the law, and the law called Mr. Barker, and eventually Mrs. Barker went to the state home for a few months and all the kids were shipped off to different relatives. The baby hadn't been hurt. She'd only been in the oven for a few minutes before we got there. But I'll never forget the way my mama handled that lady and I suppose I've even used her technique a few times in the years since. But I could've used her now for sure.

I wondered, as I sat on the plane trying not to think how far down the ground was, if Jewel was anything like Mama. If Jewel made her children laugh so hard they had to hold their stomachs, if Jewel chased her kids out in the yard with a broom threatening to rip their heads off and tell God they died in their sleep. I sat there drinking those little bitty bottles of booze and wondering. And aching. I hadn't thought of Mama in a long time. To my shame. Nor had I thought a whole bunch about my sister.

My sister. Jewel Anne Kovak Hotchkiss. The last time I'd talked to her was right after my divorce when I'd needed somebody to tell me I wasn't a scumbucket. Jewel hadn't fitted the bill on that one. To her, I'd always been a scumbucket. Ever since I'd talked her into marrying Henry Hotchkiss in the first place.

We'd never been particularly close, me and Jewel. I had been thirteen when she was born and I hadn't liked it a bit. For one thing, it was embarrassing to have a pregnant mother when you're that age. For another, I'd had my parents all to myself for thirteen years. And then she came along.

Pretty and tiny and sweet and she just made me look all the more awkward. I hadn't really paid much attention to her and when I left home she was barely five years old. I hadn't had much to do with her until Daddy died. I'd already been with the Sheriff's Department for about a year and Jewel was in her third year of college at Norman when Daddy passed on and she had rebelled in the only way girls had of doing in those days. She got pregnant. And I did something I wished I'd never done.

She called me and told me because she was afraid and didn't know what to do. And I was her big brother. So, for the first time in our relationship, I did something. I went to Norman and told her she had to marry the boy for Mama's sake. Mama couldn't take it, I'd told her. Not this on top of Daddy dying. The only decent thing for Jewel to do, I told her, was marry the boy. I was a real pompous ass about it too. It's one of those memories you have that you try not to think about. You know, the ones that sneak up on you on dark nights when you're all alone and instead of counting blessings, you start counting all the times in your life you've been a fool.

The boy that knocked up my baby sister had been Henry Hotchkiss, I guess the easiest guy at the school to seduce. Because he wasn't much else. Myopic, small, with a tremor in his hand when he shook mine. And she didn't love him and she didn't want to marry him. She just wanted it all to go away.

But I'd said no. She had to marry him. And I guess because Daddy was dead and I was the only male authority figure she had, she did it.

I'd always thought it had worked out okay, though. I'd always thought that even though I'd done that stupid thing, it'd worked out. Married for sixteen years, with three kids, Henry with a good job as an accountant for an oil company. On the outside things looked like they were okay. But I guess they weren't. Maybe who she should've shot was me.

I arrived in Houston drunk out of my mind at ten in the morning. Which didn't impress Lincoln-David-Sergeant one bit.

Instead of calling a cab, I'd called Sergeant Lincoln. I'm not sure why. Maybe one reason was that I'd written down his phone number but had forgotten to write down my sister's address. As I'd never been to Houston to visit her and as I'd never written her save birthday and Christmas cards, I didn't know her address. So he met me at the airport and didn't like what he saw. But who can blame him?

"I don't like to fly," I told him.

He just looked at me.

"I don't usually drink like this."

He turned and expected me to follow, which I did, hopping a little to keep up.

"All I ever drink is light beer. I'm not used to hard liquor."

He still didn't say anything.

"I think I gotta pee."

He stopped and looked at me for a minute, then said, "You'd think a body would know whether or not he had to pee."

I nodded my head. "Yeah, you'd think that, wouldn't ya?"

He grabbed my arm and led me to the men's room where I spent a good deal of time trying to figure out my zipper. This wasn't one of my more gracious introductions.

After I reinvented the zipper to get everything back where it belonged, we headed for the airport coffee shop where he poured two potfuls of coffee down me. I began to sober up a little.

For some reason, I took out my badge and ID and showed them to him. I guess I figured being a fellow police officer would help my present situation. He looked at them and I looked at him. He was younger than me, but shit, who isn't? Somewhere between thirty and thirty-five. He was taller than me, probably six foot two or three, with hair so blond that if he'd lived where I lived he would've been called "Cotton."

"What'd they call you when you were little?" I asked.

He grinned. "Cotton."

I grinned. "Where you from?"

"Wimberly, Texas. Little bitty old place."

"Sorry about being so drunk when I got off the plane."

"Man can't drink after what I told you, then I guess there's no real reason for liquor in this world."

"That's the God's truth."

He finished his coffee in one gulp and said, "But we need to be getting to your sister's house. Somebody from Social Services is supposed to be bringing the kids home this morning. You ready to face them?"

I took my own long gulp of coffee. "Ready as I'll ever be. Oh, by the way, you get ahold of Henry's mama?"

Lincoln gave me a wide-eyed look. "According to the kids, you're the only living relative they know about. Both grandmothers have been dead for years."

So we got up and went to his car and drove to my sister's house. With me thinking the whole way about my last conversation with Jewel. In some attempt at rekindling a brother-sister relationship that never had been, I'd tried inviting myself to Houston, tried inviting her and her family to Longbranch for Christmas. She said they couldn't come. She said Henry's mother would be visiting. But Henry's mother, according to Jewel's children, was long dead. Did my baby sister hate me so much she lied to keep away from me? I guess she did. And I guess she had her reasons. Or was it hate so much as indifference? Maybe hate would have been better. Because I'm not even sure if indifference is an emotion.

TWO

As we got my bags and headed out of the airport, I was put in mind of the one and only other time I'd been to Houston. Actually, just to the airport, and not even this one but the old one. It had been to pick up a prisoner to take back to Prophesy County. I was met by a uniformed policeman at the airport and had the prisoner handed over to me right there. This was back in the early seventies, not long after I'd joined the department. I'll never forget it either.

His name was Albert Simms and he was wanted for first-degree murder. According to the then county prosecutor who had illusions of becoming governor, seventy-five-year-old Mr. Simms had committed his most heinous of crimes against his own beloved wife, Mrs. Ruth Simms. And had to pay the highest penalty for it.

Old Albert had saved up the sleeping pills his wife's doctor had prescribed and had slipped a handful of 'em to her during the worst stage of her cancer. She had died peacefully and with a little bit of dignity, to my way of thinking. 'Course, I wasn't planning on running for governor. Mr. Simms had outlived any family that would have been in a mind to help him.

When the deputies came to the door, old Albert was in his T-shirt. So, on seeing the warrant for his arrest, he'd excused himself to get a shirt to put on out of the bedroom, but instead climbed out the window and drove his '52 Plymouth southward. Only to get pulled over for driving under the posted speed on a Houston freeway three weeks later.

After the Houston policeman had left us, Mr. Simms said he had to go to the bathroom. So I let him go. Alone. Then took myself on down a ways to a coffee shop and sat with my back facing the bathroom door. And made up some dialogue in my mind about how the conversation would go with Sheriff Blankenship when I got back home.

"Well, Sheriff, you see, the old guy was just too foxy for me. He just plain slipped one over on me, Sheriff."

But I had had my fantasy interrupted by a tap on the shoulder. "You ready, Deputy?"

I'd looked up to see Mr. Simms standing there. I took a long sip of my coffee then said, "Sure thing, Mr. Simms."

And we'd gotten on the plane together. That was one of the few times in my life I'd willingly tried to break the law, and Mr. Simms wasn't gonna let me. I figured he was probably just plain tired of the fugitive lifestyle.

On the plane he talked a lot about his late wife. "Married forty-seven years this August," he'd said. "Only woman I ever looked at my whole life. Sweet little woman, my Ruthie. Used to say, 'Bertie...' she called me Bertie..."

"Yes, sir."

"Used to say, 'Bertie, I'm still so glad I married you.' Even to the end she said that. She said, 'Bertie, it hurts so much, Bertie...' I just couldn't let her go on like that, Deputy."

"Yes, sir," I'd said and patted his hand. I heard two years later he'd died of cancer of the lymph nodes in a prison hospital, with nobody around to help him end it with any kind of dignity.

As we got in Sergeant Lincoln's car and left the airport, finagling our way onto the freeway, I started looking out the window at this city that had been Jewel's home for ten years. Houston, Texas. God, what a pit. The ride was mile after mile of fast-food joints, small dying businesses, and used-car lots. Lots and lots of used-car lots. The air outside and inside the car was heavy with moisture and something I wasn't quite sure of. The sky was a putrid shade of gray and there was a haze over everything. I supposed that this was what smog was all about.

It wasn't as cold probably as it had been back home, the temperature said it was only in the mid-fifties for this second week of February. But it felt cold. Wet cold. The sergeant's car heater didn't do anything to dispel that feeling. But the cold wasn't just wind chill, it was heart chill, if there is such a thing. Not knowing what's happening, walking into the kind of situation I was walking into, put a chill on your heart.

"You and your sister real close, Mr. Kovak?" Sergeant Lincoln asked, breaking into my cold thoughts.

"Not what you'd call close," I hedged, not willing to say, "Actually, she hates my guts and I can't remember her children's names."

"Well, I got me three sisters, Mr. Kovak, and I sure as the devil would know how I'd feel right now. I sure am sorry about all this."

"I appreciate that," I said. We were silent after that, both thinking about our sisters, I suppose. I only hoped he had more pleasant memories of his than I had of mine. Any memories at all, I guess, would have been an improvement.

It seemed as if it took hours to get to Jewel's house, and maybe it did. The traffic was terrible.

You can talk about the Los Angeles freeways and
the traffic jams at Times Square, but you haven't
seen anything until you've been on a Houston
freeway in rush hour with bumper-to-bumper traffic all going seventy miles an hour. It'll scare the
dog piss out of you. And a Houston rush hour
seems to start around six in the morning and end
around eleven at night.

As we drove around the city on the freeways, I
kept seeing downtown. Even after we'd passed it.
That damned city has more downtowns than it
oughta, and that's the God's truth. We finally got
off the freeway in the southwest part of town, the
exact opposite end of town from the airport, and
drove over potholed streets full of construction
equipment and way too many cars. I kept remem-
bering all the newscasts I'd heard about what a dying city Houston was. How everybody was moving
out. You sure as hell couldn't tell that by the cars.

But as we drove through the upper-middle-class
residential area where Jewel lived, I began to see
signs of it. Mid-February and there were empty
houses with knee-high grass and weeds. No telling
how many summers they'd sat empty with no one
to tend the yards. On every block, at least two
houses had that look. That empty, nobody-loves-
me look. Weeds waist high, gutters full of years of

leaves, shutters losing paint and hinges, garage doors hanging at an angle, newspapers in hard, sodden balls in the driveway.

The houses that weren't empty looked nice enough, though. I imagined that at one time, when Houston was the high-rolling city it was meant to be, that this was a prime piece of real estate. An expensive neighborhood maybe. The houses were all about twenty years old, built sometime in the late sixties.

We pulled into Jewel's driveway and I almost cried. The house looked like the people who lived there loved it. Trim, winter-dead lawn, a basketball hoop over the garage doors, two well-kept trees in the front yard, and a mat at the front door with a smiley face and the name "Hotchkiss" stenciled on it. In the driveway was a Volkswagen with big wheels and no fenders, painted a bright yellow, and a ten-speed girl's bike.

It was a home with children, a home made by my sister and her husband, a home that told the world it was full of love. But what had been going on inside? Inside the house and inside my sister? Maybe, God forbid, I'd never know.

Sergeant Lincoln had a key to the front door and let us in. The inside of the house let me know my mama had done a good job of raising Jewel. It looked just like Mama's house. I figured in a pinch you could eat off the commode seat. It was that clean. There was a small hall as we entered, with a living room going off to the left. The furniture in the living room wasn't old and it wasn't new, just good. If I had to guess, I'd say it was what they call "traditional" and all of it matched, with a few pieces of what looked like real antique mixed in for flavor, and there was a well-polished, baby grand piano in a place of honor, reminding me of the times I'd go back to my parents' home, after I'd moved out, and hear little Jewel banging away at some Godawful tune or another on the old upright. Mama had invited the wife and me to a recital of Jewel's one time, when she was in high school, but, being the brother I was, I didn't go.

There was a dining alcove at the end of the living room with a well-polished dark wood table and chairs and hutch of some sort and built-in china cabinets in the corners. I could see Mama's china set gleaming in the cabinets. To the left of the entry was the hall that led to the bedrooms, four in all, if you counted the one that was obviously Henry's office. There were two bathrooms, one off the hall and the master bath.

The entry hall itself emptied into the den, at the far left of which was the kitchen, separated from

the den by a bar with a stained-glass window that
slid up into the wall. Every room was immaculate,
even the kids' rooms. I figured Jewel to be one of
those kinds of mamas. Like our mama. "A cluttered room shows a cluttered mind, Milton." That's
what Mama used to say. And I could almost hear
Jewel telling her kids the same thing.

Yeah, everything was immaculate, until you got
to the den. The den, with its built-in bookshelves
neatly packed with bright colored books, a living
room suite just a little older than the one in the
front room, a big-screen TV set, a decent stereo
system, a fireplace that looked so clean you wondered if it had ever been used, and one wall
crammed with pictures; pictures of all three children at different stages of life; pictures of Jewel and
Henry on a fishing trip holding a fish larger than
my sister; Jewel and Henry in Hawaii with leis
around their necks and drinks with little parasols in
their hands; Jewel and Henry at a podium where
Henry was being honored for something or other.

Yeah, the den matched the rest of the house except for one thing. The big, brownish red stain in
the middle of the Oriental rug. And the chalk outline of my brother-in-law's body. Somehow, I just
couldn't see Jewel dirtying her house like this. If she

had to do this, I figured she'd go out in the back-yard.

"You through with this?" I asked Lincoln, in-dicating the rug.

"Yeah."

I moved the coffee table off the rug and pulled the part of it that was under the legs of the couch out and rolled it up. He helped me and we man-aged to get the rug out of the room, out of the house, and into the garage. When we got back, there was still a bit of a stain on the hardwood floor. I went to the hall bathroom and took the bathmat and brought it into the den, placing it over the stain then putting the coffee table on top of the bathmat. It didn't look too bad. It almost looked natural, even if the coffee table wasn't exactly cen-tered.

And then the doorbell rang and I braced myself for my baby sister's children. The last time I'd seen Jewel's kids had been three years before at Mama's funeral. Though I hadn't really seen much of them then. Henry had kept them out of the way most of the time, letting Jewel and I get on with the busi-ness of burying our mother. I had to think real hard to even remember their names. Leonard, the old-est, Marlene, the girl in the middle, and Carl, the baby.

When I opened the front door, the three of them were standing there in their winter coats with a middle-aged lady who held out her hand for me to shake and introduced herself as Ms. Kemper, the social worker from Social Services. She was very, very cheerful.

I led them into the den where we all stood around awkwardly staring at each other while Ms. Kemper and Sergeant Lincoln talked, as if we weren't even there. Finally, with requests from both that I call immediately if I needed anything, the sergeant and the social worker left.

I stood at the front door after I'd closed it, leaning my head against it, not wanting to walk back into that den where my baby sister had killed her husband and where her children now stood. I didn't know what to do. I had no real practice in dealing with kids, and hadn't the slightest idea what to do with my own niece and nephews. Finally, I turned and walked back into the den.

Carl and Leonard were squatting on the floor, the coffee table pushed back, the bathmat lifted.

"Well, it's not too bad," Leonard said.

"You'd think there'd be more blood," answered his little brother.

Marlene was on the couch, knees up Indian fashion. "Jeeze, you two are gross."

When they saw me, they all three had the grace to blush. And Leonard managed to get the bathmat and coffee table back in place. I sat down on the couch with Marlene while the boys picked the two chairs and we just sat there, them staring at me and me staring at them.

"Now what?" Leonard asked.

Well, he had me for sure on that one. Now what, indeed. "Lunch?" I suggested and they all agreed. Like my mama used to say, when in doubt, eat.

There was bologna, white bread, and potato chips and we had ourselves a little mini-feast. While we sat around the bar eating our sandwiches and drinking glasses of milk, I decided I'd better get it over with.

"So, can ya'll tell me what happened?"

Carl and Marlene looked at each other and Leonard shrugged. With a mouthful of sandwich, the eldest said, "Shit if I know. We just came home and there they were."

"They fight a lot?" I asked.

Carl and Marlene looked at each other and Leonard shrugged. "Naw. Hardly ever."

"Anything happen lately out of the ordinary?"

Carl and Marlene looked at each other and Leonard shrugged. "Naw. Same old shit."

Finally I said, "Your mama know you got a garbage mouth?"

Carl and Marlene looked at each other and burst out laughing. Marlene said, "If Mama heard him talking like that, she'd stick a whole bar of Dial right down his stupid throat!"

"Why don't you just shut your face, you prissymouth bitch!"

"Yeah? And who's gonna make me, weinerhole? You?"

I managed to get between them before they did any real maiming and mutilating and silently thanked my parents for waiting thirteen years between me and Jewel. At least we never had to go through this. Carl, the youngest, just sat there quietly eating his sandwich and not paying any attention to his siblings.

Strangely enough, though, the two stopped as quickly as they started and both finished their lunches, talking with their mouths full about some damned TV program. Kids, I swear to God. And if Jewel didn't make... Well, I wasn't gonna think about that now.

We managed to get through the rest of the day thanks to the TV set. What with cable and their stock of VCR-taped movies, they could stay in gaga land indefinitely. The phone rang a few times, once Jewel and Henry's preacher wanting to know what he could do to help. I told him I didn't know right then, but asked for his phone number just in case. He said he'd go by and see Jewel, which was something I knew I'd have to do sooner or later. As she was still in a coma, and I was still a coward, I figured later was better. Another call came from a woman who knew Jewel from Carl's PTA. I got the impression she didn't know Jewel all that well either. And all she wanted to do was ask questions. Probably so she could go back to the PTA and be the fountain of news. She didn't get any from me.

And there was a call from another woman, this one a neighbor whose kids carpooled with Jewel's.

"I hope you don't mind me calling, Mr...ah..."

"Kovak."

"Mr. Kovak. I just wanted to let you know that I'm right down the street if you need anything. And don't worry about food. I'm working on that now. I'll be bringing dinner over tonight and I've got a couple of other neighbors working on tomorrow...."

"You don't have to do that, ma'am, I'm plenty capable of cooking...."

"Well, Mr. Kovak, I figure you've got other things on your mind right now. And...well, I just want to do something. Jewel...well, I didn't know her all that well, but...anyway, I just want to help.''

I thanked her and when she showed up later that evening with dinner, I accepted it and thanked her again. And I got to thinking about people. They can do the strangest things. One minute they can be Godawful pricks and the next they can do something that makes a grown man want to burst into tears. Some grown men, not me, of course. Hey, I'm a sensitive guy, but I don't need to prove it!

The way I figure it, all people got their mean spots. One of the nicest guys I ever knew in my life, the kind of guy that wouldn't just give you the shirt off his back, he'd launder it first, was the biggest bigot I'd ever seen. And I had a teacher in the fourth grade, meanest woman who ever lived. She'd slap your hand with a ruler so hard that when you died at one hundred and three, or whenever, you'd be explaining the scar to God. One day I saw her out in the school yard picking up a bird with a broken wing and carefully putting it in her car. One of the guys said she was probably taking it home to fry, but I doubted it.

The people in my hometown were like that. Good and bad. Mean and sweet. Sometimes both at the same time. But when there was a death, no matter what the circumstances, they were there for the survivors. And I guessed that people in a big city like Houston weren't all that different from the people in my hometown. Except this one couldn't cook worth a damn.

Later that night, after the kids went off to their rooms, I sat in the den and wondered why no friends had called. The lady from the PTA admitted not being close to Jewel, and so did the lady that brought the food. Jewel and Henry had lived in Houston for ten years. Where were their friends? I thought about asking the kids, but somehow, I didn't want to.

Finally, around nine, I got up and went to the boys' room. Leonard was looking at a magazine that he stashed the minute I walked in, making me wonder about its contents, and Carl was watching a little Sony TV, no bigger than a radio.

"Hey, boys," I said.

They both nodded but didn't say much. "What time's bedtime around here?"

"Depends on whether or not we're going to church in the morning," Leonard answered.

The boy had a point. "Guess maybe it's be a good idea if ya'll stayed home," I ventured, "what with us having to go to the hospital and see your mama and all."

Leonard shrugged and Carl looked away. "Whatever," Leonard said.

"Well, why don't ya'll go on now and take your baths, you first, Carl, okay? And we can get that out of the way."

"Whatever," Carl said.

"Okay, then, why don't you do that?"

He shrugged and I left their room and headed across the hall to Marlene's. She was on the phone, which she hung up quick and I could tell by the way her eyes looked and her voice sounded that she'd been crying. Jesus help me, I didn't know how to handle this. Not at all. What the hell do you do for a fourteen-year-old girl whose whole life was crumbling around her?

I sat down on the bed next to her. "I got Carl taking his bath now," I said. The clear sound of running water came through the wall that connected her room to the hall bath. "Why don't you take yours next and then Leonard? Is that the way ya'll do it?"

She looked at her toes and shrugged. "Yeah, that's fine."

"Marlene, I don't wanna disrupt things any more than they already been. So you just tell me if I'm doing something wrong, okay?"

She nodded her head, which was still pointed at her toes. I patted her shoulder because I didn't know what else to do and left the room.

By ten o'clock baths were taken and they were in their rooms all squeaky-clean with the promise to turn off their lights before much longer, and it was my turn. I got my bag and took it back to the master bedroom and set it on the bed, then walked to the door of the master bath and turned on the light.

The bathroom was like the rest of the house, neat as a pin, and there were two silver trays on the long double-sink counter, one with perfumes and lotions and such, the other holding a bottle of Aqua Velva, some deodorant, and an electric razor. Toothbrushes hung side by side next to a Dixie Cup dispenser, one blue and one yellow, and monogrammed towels were on a towel rack next to the tub. Behind the door two robes were on two hooks. One was navy blue terrycloth and the other was white silk. I touched the silk and as it swung from my touch, I saw an appliquéd butterfly on the back and smelled a sweet scent.

I turned off the light and walked to the bed and picked up my suitcase, turned off the light in the bedroom, closing the door behind me, and took my bag into the den. I didn't belong in my sister's bedroom. No one did but Jewel and Henry. 'Course, now no one but Jewel belonged there. Maybe, God forbid, not even her.

I took my shower in the hall bath, found some sheets, a blanket, and a pillow in the hall closet and made my bed on the couch in the den. However long it took for my sister to get well and me to get the hell back to Oklahoma was gonna seem even longer than it was, backache-wise. But I'm not complaining.

It was a long night. Part of it, of course, was the hum. That Godawful city hum you don't hear where I come from. You don't notice it so much in the daylight, but put your head down on a pillow in a darkened room and it's louder than the second coming.

Laying on the couch where I was, in direct line to the bedroom hallway, I was aware of the long night my baby sister's children were having. At one point, the boys' door opened and I heard someone using the toilet and forgetting to flush. Later, I heard crying and couldn't tell which room it was coming from. I didn't go investigate. I'm a cop, not a shrink or a preacher, or a very good uncle. It seemed as though one of the three of them was up continually through the whole night, and when one of them was awake, I was awake. Maybe that's what all parents go through. I don't know. But it sure makes for a long night.

Sunday we didn't go to church. And somehow, we never got around to going to the hospital. I didn't mention it because I'm a coward, the kids didn't mention it because . . . I got a call from Sergeant Lincoln telling me Henry's body would be released for burial come Wednesday. I thanked him and got out the telephone book and looked up funeral homes. I wrote a list of ones that looked like they might be close by and decided come Monday morning I'd do a little comparison shopping. God only knew how long it would be before any checking and savings accounts of Jewel and Henry's would be available to me. And my funds were limited. Especially after me buying the house and all.

At some point I figured I should start worrying about the kids' nutrition, since after only one day of it, I was already a little sick of cold cereal for breakfast, sandwiches for lunch, and the slop the ladies of the neighborhood brought over for dinner, which seemed not to have a vegetable anywhere near it. But I figured I could put that worry off for a little while.

The kids stayed in front of the TV most of the day, with the boys taking a break right after lunch to go shoot some baskets in the driveway. Which left Marlene and me alone.

"You wanna talk?" I asked her.

"About what?"

"You know."

"Naw. I don't want to talk about it." She shrugged and went and turned on the TV. I figured something was going to have to break for these kids pretty soon. They were stiff-upper-lipping it all over the place, but at some point they'd break. The social worker had given me her card, and I thought maybe tomorrow, between calling funeral homes, I'd better check in with her and see if she had any ideas. And then I stopped thinking and started watching the TV. Because even an uncle needs a release every once in a while.

The boys came back in and we all just sat there and watched the TV, pretending life was all right. And that's when Honey showed up.

The back door opened with a bang and a Southern belle voice chirped, "Jewel Anne? We're back!"

And all three kids jumped up, burst into tears, and ran into the arms of the lady standing in the kitchen. Who looked at me, shoved the kids behind her, and said, "Who the hell are you?"

"I'm Jewel's brother, Milton. Milton Kovak."

The lady smiled real big and held out her hand. "Oh, hi! I've heard of you! I'm Honey Lancaster from next door. What's wrong with the kids?"

And then we all started talking at once, me and the kids. For some reason, this lady was going to make everything all right. I knew it and the kids knew it. So finally, between the four of us, we got the story out.

"My God, Henry's dead?" A tear fell down her cheek. She hugged the kids to her. "You poor babies!" She looked at me. "Is Jewel okay? No, of course she isn't. Not if she's in a coma. And the stupid police think what? That Jewel shot Henry? Well, it's a goddamn lie!" she said. "I don't care what it looks like, Jewel Anne Hotchkiss didn't kill anybody and I'll kill anybody says she did!"

"That's what we've been trying to tell everybody!" Carl wailed. Funny, he hadn't mentioned it to me. Funny, they hadn't mentioned a goddamn thing to me.

"Well, Honey's here," Honey said, "and Honey's gonna straighten it out. Don't you worry." And all three kids, even six-foot Leonard, held on to the lady next door and let her treat them like the kids in need they were.

Let me describe Honey. If I can. She was about Jewel's age, thirty-five or thereabouts, and she had hair the color of my mama's butterscotch pudding. Not just anybody's butterscotch pudding, but my mama's butterscotch pudding. Because Mama never did get it stirred just right and it always had these streaks of milk running through it. That's what Honey's hair looked like, butterscotch pudding with streaks of milk. Her skin, even for the winter, was this deep, rich beige tone, the same shade as the darker parts of her hair, and her eyes were a light, golden brown, giving her the effect of being the same color all over—hair, skin, and eyes. Honey wasn't just a name, it was a description.

She was about five foot nothing and what some people who think of Cheryl Tiegs as a fine figure of a woman would call fat, but actually, she was just right. Well proportioned, with a tiny waist and breasts and hips that seemed to match. She had this overbite, just a little one, reminding me of Jean Tierney, the first actress ever to wake up the old gene pool. And when she smiled, she lit up the whole room. I had this overwhelming urge to join the kids in their huddle around her.

But then the back door opened again and a booming voice, "Hey, Henry, where the fuck are you?"

"Chuck! Watch your mouth!" Honey hollered back, and the boys left her and ran to the man who entered and threw their arms around him.

"What the fuck's going on? Lenny? Carl?"

So we went through the whole story again, with Honey again denying that Jewel Anne had done what it only looked like she'd done. Chuck, if you'll excuse the expression, was dumbfounded. "Henry? Dead? Naw! Come on, ya'll, this ain't fucking funny!"

We all assured him it was true and Honey introduced Chuck to me. He was her husband, which I had already figured out. He was about a foot and a half taller than her, weighed about two seventy-five, and had absolutely no neck, just a gold chain to indicate where one would go if he had one. And when he shook my hand, I was afraid the feeling in my fingers would never come back. And the boy had hair. Lots of it. Thick, dark, and styled.

"So who the fuck says Jewel Anne did this, anyway?" He looked at me as if daring me to say I thought she might have done it. I'm not that stupid.

"The police, and the social worker, and the newspapers, and everybody," wailed Marlene, who still held on to Honey.

"Well, fuck the bunch of 'em," Chuck said. "Because I know like I know my own name that Jewel Anne fuckin' well didn't do no such thing."

"Watch your language," Honey said. I figured this was one of those hiccups of speech you read about. "You kids go on now and let Chuck and me talk to your Uncle Milton. We gotta figure out what we're gonna do."

So the kids hugged everybody but me and went to their rooms. And I sat on the sofa looking at Honey sitting in a chair and Chuck sitting on the coffee table and worried about the coffee table and Jewel's household insurance.

"So Henry's dead?" Chuck asked, sitting on the coffee table and shaking his head. "That's fucking depressing."

"So how they been getting on?" I asked, and Chuck glared at me.

"They got on just fine, Milt! I swear to you!" Honey said. "They had their little squabbles, but who doesn't?"

"The kids said they never fought at all."

"Yeah," Chuck said, "well, that was Henry. He didn't believe in fucking around in front of the kids. No fighting, ya know? He said if they hadda fucking fight, they'd fuckin' well do it behind closed fuckin' doors, ya know?"

"Look," Honey said, leaning toward me with this cute, little earnest look about her, "you didn't know Jewel Anne. I know she's your sister and all, but I happen to know you two weren't close and you just didn't know her at all. Jewel Anne could no more kill Henry than she could sprout wings and fly."

She held up a hand as if stopping me from saying something which I hadn't been about to say. "I know, you're a police officer and you figure everybody says that about everybody else. All these neighbors that say about mass murderers, 'Well, he was just the nicest fella, so quiet...'" Her voice was doing a high falsetto. "Well, forget that shit! Jewel Anne was my closest friend and I knew her! I knew her better than Henry did! There's only one reason she'd strike out at Henry and that would be if he was messing with the kids. And he wasn't. He never even spanked them. So, I'm telling you, she didn't do this. And another thing...where did it happen?"

I told her and she shoved at Chuck who stood up and picked up the coffee table like some of us pick up sticks, and she removed the bathmat that covered the blood stain.

"Well, that tears it!" Honey said. "I had no doubts to begin with, but this proves it beyond a shadow of a doubt! If she did it, she wouldn't do it in her house! Jewel Anne dirty her house up like this? Not on your life!'' I remembered I'd vaguely thought something along those same lines myself but just nodded my head.

"Fuckin' A!" Chuck said in agreement with his wife, still standing there holding the coffee table and staring down at the stain. "Jewel Anne was real neat. She'd a done it in the garage with a drop cloth."

"Well?" Honey asked me, a challenge of some sort.

"You're right," I said. "But if Jewel didn't do this, then who did?"

Chuck put down the coffee table and sat back down on it and Honey sat down in her chair. They looked at each other then at me. Finally, Honey said, "Well, we're just gonna have to find out, now aren't we?"

THREE

WELL, IT TURNED OUT Chuck was good for more than picking up coffee tables. It turned out that he was Jewel and Henry's insurance man. Something he got into as a sideline during his first and only year with the Houston Oilers. Right before they cut him loose after a knee injury that never healed properly.

I had a little fantasy about Chuck selling insurance to an unsuspecting buyer.

Chuck: "You gonna fuckin' well buy this fuckin' insurance or what?"

Buyer: "Yes, sir, right away, sir."

So Chuck was gonna fix up everything, insurance-wise.

"I made sure Henry got homeowner's insurance, with a death clause, so the house'll be free and clear. 'Course, right now that's as fuckin' lucky as a virgin with herpes. Same death clause with both cars, but those you can probably sell. His life insurance policy is for five hundred thousand dollars. Though I'm not sure about murder. And what with them suspecting Jewel Anne . . . well, I'll have

to check into that. The kids are the second benefi-
ciaries, so that should work out. Hospitalization,
though, is through Henry's company. I'll give 'em
a call for you, make sure they're not trying to screw
Jewel Anne." I smiled to myself thinking about the
fate of any little old insurance clerk dumb enough
to try to screw my sister out of her hospitalization
with Chuck around. "And I'll get in touch with
Henry's lawyer. He's mine too. See what we can do
about releasing some coin."

I nodded my head in agreement, afraid that if I
spoke I'd end up sounding like the broke slob I was.

"Now," said Honey, "about funeral homes for
Henry..."

I showed her my list and she immediately started
crossing off names.

"This guy's active on a committee to ban school
books, he's not getting our business...and this guy,
well, he's a big supporter of the Contras, saw that
in the paper when the shit hit the fan awhile
back...and this is a big conglomerate with hold-
ings in South Africa...can't use them. Okay, here's
one I don't know a thing about."

"Watch it now," Chuck said, "I hear this guy
eats grapes," and he burst out laughing.

By the look she gave him, I could tell Honey
didn't find it amusing.

Chuck shrugged and grinned sheepishly. "Ah, babe, I'm sorry. I was just fuckin' around, ya know?"

"Well, we've got 'till Wednesday to figure out who we want to use," I said. "I'll leave that up to you, Honey, if that's okay?"

She patted my arm with her tiny hand. "You don't worry about it, Milton. I'll find the right person."

Their leave-taking was a bit awkward. I thought for a minute there Honey was gonna kiss me, but finally she just squeezed my hand and Chuck patted my shoulder like some heavyweights pat their opponents and they left the way they'd come, through the back door. By that time, it was way past eight so I just sat for a while, pretending I was all alone and not having to do anything but just sit and contemplate my navel, or whatever. I did my rounds in the kids' rooms again, letting them know that going to school the next day was something they didn't have to think about. For some reason, maybe time, more probably the fact that Honey was available to them, the kids slept better that night. I noticed because the hum had me up half the night, and I was all alone.

On Monday morning, with Chuck off to work, Honey drove the kids and me to the hospital to see

Jewel. I'd called the two schools the three kids went to (Carl to the junior high and Leonard and Marlene to the high school) and explained the situation. The junior high lady who answered the phone already knew all about it, probably from the PTA lady, I figured, but I had to go into detail at the high school. The secretary there was real nice, said she'd explain to both kids' teachers and have some friends bring home any assignments so that Leonard and Marlene wouldn't get behind. I didn't know at this point how long I'd keep them out of school. Just something else I was going to have to play by ear.

Ben Taub Hospital is the emergency hospital for Houston and it isn't the nicest place in the world. Even on this Monday morning, there were people walking the halls with bloody heads and broken bodies, wandering around in a drunken stupor. I guess with unemployment as high as it is in Houston, Monday morning isn't much different than Saturday night.

The hospital was located in what Houston likes to boast of as their Medical Center, which is about a million hospitals all crammed together and landscaped with high-rise parking garages that would like to take your car hostage and only release it after you'd arranged for a government loan to bail it out.

Jewel was in a private room with a police guard. I swear to God. My little sister under police guard. Laying there unconscious with a pimply faced kid in a uniform there to make sure she didn't walk in her sleep, I suppose. He didn't want to at first, but after I showed him my badge and ID, he let us all in. The nurses weren't thrilled about it either, but Honey took care of them. Somehow, I figured taking on Honey would be even harder than taking on Chuck. For so small a lady, she was what you might call a formidable woman.

I might have mentioned that Jewel had been a pretty baby. Well, she was a pretty child, too, and up until last Friday, I suppose, she was a pretty woman. She had that kind of golden blonde hair that no chemist could ever put in a bottle, green eyes so bright they looked like emeralds, and skin the color of peaches and cream. And even after the three kids, her figure was still nice and trim.

Well, that was up until Friday. Now laying there in that hospital bed with tubes running out of her nose and her arm and everywhere else, she just didn't look like Jewel. What she looked like was Mama, about a week before she passed on. Her skin was gray, curdled cream with the peaches long gone. The hair had lost the shine it always had and the lids of her eyes were closed over the emerald sparkle.

I could hear the kids sniffing behind me but didn't turn around. Because if I did, I'd probably start sniffing too.

But Honey, well, Honey just walked right up to the bed and said, "Hey, Jewel Anne! We're here! How you doing? Guess who I've got with me? Your brother, Milton. Milton, say hi to Jewel Anne."

I looked at Honey for a minute, then at my sister lying there in a coma. "Hey, Jewel," I said, "how you doing?"

"Milton's come to look after the kids so don't you worry about anything except getting better, okay? The kids are here. Children, say hi to your mama."

So the kids went through the ritual of saying hi to a woman who didn't even know they were there. Except for Leonard. He stared hard at Honey and said, "She can't hear us. Why are you making us do this?"

Honey walked up to the boy, leaning her head back to peer up into his face, and grabbed the front of his shirt. "You say hi to your mama and you say it now, boy."

"Hey, Mama."

Honey walked over to the bed and sat on the side of it. "Jewel Anne, we got a problem only you can help us with. They say you killed Henry. Can you believe that shit? I told them they were full of it, but you know the stupid cops. They'd need both hands and a flashlight to find their asses in the dark! So anyway, you gotta come out of the coma so you can tell us what happened, Jewel Anne. That's probably the only way we're gonna know who did it." She laughed and said, "You're not gonna believe some of the phone calls Milton's been getting! That woman, Martha Davenport, on the junior high PTA, well..."

And she went on and on, telling her about the vacation she and Chuck had just come back from, and everything and anything else she could think of. After a while, the kids and I wandered out of the room and went down to the cafeteria to eat. Honey joined us after about an hour and I left her with the kids and went in search of Jewel's doctor.

He was a resident named something or other Hussain and his accent was so thick that a nurse finally started interpreting for me. Basically, what he said was that the longer Jewel stayed in a coma, the worse her chances of coming out of it. He said the bullet had entered her skull at the top left quadrant and had lodged against some lobe or another. They had operated and removed the bullet. If she did regain consciousness, though, one of several things could result. Permanent or partial paralysis, total or partial loss of memory, or total or partial catatonia. In other words, even if she lived, my baby sister could be a vegetable for the rest of her life.

I left the doctor and went back to the cafeteria, feeling like stepped-in dog shit.

On the way home from the hospital Honey stopped at a bookstore where we all had to buy a book that we would personally read to Jewel. I was surprised when Marlene picked out *Anne of Green Gables*. She said that had been her mama's favorite book as a child. I thought it was a sign of the kind of brother I was that I didn't know my sister's favorite book.

I picked up the newest Michener, not because he was Jewel's favorite writer or anything, but because he was mine. See, that's the kind of brother I am. And Honey, well, Honey was picking up every self-help book in the place, and a Spanish-language tape.

"Jewel Anne's always wanted to learn Spanish," she said.

And that's the way the week went, us going to the hospital every day, taking turns reading our books, or sitting in the cafeteria, and, as we left each day,

Honey would turn on the tape recorder she brought and put the ear plugs for it in Jewel's ears and turn on the Spanish tapes.

"She might as well learn something while she's just lying there," Honey explained.

Other than going to the hospital every day, the rest of the week just sorta happened. The ladies in the neighborhood kept on bringing food over, and on Wednesday we got Henry's body to a funeral home where the owner had voted a straight Democratic ticket for the last thirty years, and on Friday, we buried Henry. It was a closed service presided over by Jewel and Henry's preacher with just the Lancasters, me and the kids, and Henry's boss and secretary in attendance.

That afternoon, Chuck said I'd better talk to Henry's lawyer because the insurance company handling the life insurance was going to play hard ball.

On Saturday, I called Elberry Blankenship.

"Hey, boy, how are you?" he said when I finally got through all the well-wishing from Gladys, our front desk clerk, and two of the deputies who hadda get on the line to say hidy. Dalton Pettigrew, one of the deputies, was particularly upset about the whole business as he had been a year ahead of Jewel Anne in high school and had asked her out seven times, which he told me when we first met. Jewel had never gone out with him but Dalton figured that just the asking had us connected in some way.

"Sheriff, I'm thinking maybe, under the circumstances and all, it might be for the best if I just took a leave of absence."

"Boy, you got such a shitpot of sick and vacation time, we don't gotta worry none about that now."

"Well, yeah, I guess . . ."

"Now give me Jewel Anne's address so's I can mail your checks there."

I gave him the address and he said, "So how's Jewel Anne?"

"Still in a coma."

"Shit, boy, I don't like that."

"Me, neither, Sheriff."

"What happened, if you don't mind my asking?"

"We're not real sure. But the police are real happy thinking Jewel shot Henry and then shot herself."

"But you're not?"

"Now, Elberry, would you be happy with that kinda explanation if it was your kin?"

"Not hardly. But, boy," and there was silence for a moment before he said, "prepare yourself. You understand?"

I sighed. "Yes, sir, I understand."

"So what are you doing?"

"Nothing at this point. It's too early. But I'll keep you posted."

"You do that, boy."

"How's everything up home?"

"Well, Mama took a spell. Looked like her heart at first, then the doctor said it was just real bad gas. Glenda Sue's staying to your place?"

"Yeah. She's feeding the cat and watering the plant."

"You could do worse than that woman, Milton."

"Yes, sir."

And we went on for a bit more, with me worrying the whole time how I was gonna pay for the phone call.

On Monday my first check got there, having been Fed X'ed by my thoughtful boss, so I had to go through the hassle of finding a bank that would cash my paycheck from Longbranch, Oklahoma. I had to go to three banks to do it. And the one that finally cashed it I almost didn't go into because of what their sign said.

You know those computer readout-type signs banks have nowadays where they have messages for the whole world to see and they don't just stop with the time and temperature anymore? Now these signs tell you how much interest you can get on a money market account and how they're having a special on boat loans, for God's sake. Well, this one, after the commercial, said, and I'm not shitting you, *HAVE A GREAT DAY!!!* And I got pissed.

First, it was have a nice day. Isn't that enough responsibility? Sometimes, most times, it's an uphill battle having a slightly better than unpleasant day, on those days that aren't dog-shit awful, and now these assholes want me to have a great day! But I got some questions. Who's this decree coming from? And who the hell named this person, whoever the hell they might be, keeper of my day? And secondly, what *is* a great day? Or even a nice one?

For some people, winning the lottery would be a great day; for others, sometimes me included, not having open-heart surgery would do it.

And while I was worrying over my lack of a great day, Jewel just lay there in the hospital with tubes running in and out of her.

On that same Monday the kids went back to school. Carl went in his carpool with the lady down the street and Marlene and Leonard went in Leonard's Volkswagen. That afternoon, I was sitting in the den waiting for them. Carl got dropped off first. His mood was subdued and he went straight in to do his homework. I heard the VW pull into the driveway and waited. After less than a minute, Marlene came in, said hi, and shot off to her room. And I waited. No Leonard. Finally I got up and went out the back door to the driveway. Leonard was sitting in the VW, head resting on the steering wheel.

I opened the passenger side door and leaned my head in. "Boy, you okay?"

His "Yeah" was muffled and I noticed he didn't move his head to look at me.

"Leonard, you wanna look at me when I talk to you, please?" I said in my deputy voice.

"Yes, sir." He turned to face me. And the right side of that face was not a thing of beauty, let me tell you. The eye was swole shut, the cheek bruised, and his lip was busted.

I stood up away from the car. "Get out of the car, boy," I said.

He opened his door and slid out. Under the open carcoat I could see his shirt was torn and there was a hole in the knee of his pants that had nothing to do with fashion.

"Come on in the house."

"Yes, sir."

I led and he followed, with me wondering the whole time what in the hell I was gonna do about this. Play it like an uncle? Didn't know how. Play it like a cop? Only thing I knew. Once in the den, I stood aside and pointed toward the couch.

"Sit."

He sat.

"You wanna tell me what happened, Leonard?"

He shrugged and looked at the floor. His eyes unfortunately focused on the bathmat covering the bloodstain left by his father, and he quickly looked away.

I sat down on the easy chair, body bent forward, arms resting on my knees, an earnest look on my face. My "good cop" position. "Leonard, I'm not blind and I'm not stupid. I see you been hurt and I know you didn't run into any door. And these aren't injuries you can get playing in the band. You wanna tell me what's going on?"

He shrugged and looked off toward the kitchen. "Just some asshole at school."

"He just beat you up 'cause he didn't like your ugly face, or what?"

Again the shrug. I had this overwhelming urge to lay a heavy hand on his shoulder and pull his face toward me. But I'm well trained. I didn't give in to the impulse.

"Well, boy? And you shrug again, you ain't gonna have a shoulder left to shrug with."

He looked at me again. "He was talking about Mom. Saying Mom killed Daddy. Saying—it runs in the family—how I'm probably gonna be a killer too, just like Mom..."

I sighed long and hard. "Your mama didn't kill your daddy. You know that don't you, Leonard?"

He half shrugged, thought better of it, and said, "That's what I want to believe."

"Well, believe it," I said, wishing I felt as convinced as I sounded.

He squirmed around on the couch and I saw him trying to control his face, trying to stop the sobbing that was so near. "I want something to happen! I want to find out who did this! I want to kill the son of a bitch! I mean it! I want to kill him!"

I stood up and moved over to the couch, sitting down next to him and putting an arm awkwardly around his shoulders. "We're gonna find the son of a bitch, don't worry about that. And when we do, we're gonna tie him up in a pretty pink ribbon and hand him over to the police."

He pulled away from me. "I want to kill him," he said, his voice so quiet it scared the dog piss out of me.

"Boy, you listen to me . . ." I started, but he was gone, off to his room.

ON TUESDAY, after school, with Leonard's face healed nice enough to be seen in public, Honey took them shopping. While they were gone, Chuck got home from work and came over and he and I proceeded to drink up all the beer in Jewel's house and his house.

And we talked a little about his town, this piss-hole called Houston.

"Man, this used to be some sorta place, Milt. I wanna tell ya."

"Yeah?"

"Oh, yea. Great town. Lots of money. This town has a money history that'd curl your fuckin' hair."

"What's left of it."

He laughed. "Now, though, Jesus. I barely made my nut last month. Had to take a cut in my own salary, man, now tell me that ain't shit?"

"That's shit, Chuck. It truly is."

"Who in hell wants to buy insurance on a house that got repoed, though? Know what I mean? Who wants to keep up their fire insurance when they could use the money to buy groceries for their kids?''

"True."

"The fuckin' American dream's gone, Milt. I mean it."

"You may be right."

"Fuckin' A I'm right! You know all this crap you see on TV and in the movies about the fifties? All these TV shows and shit glorifying the fifties?"

"Yeah?"

"You know why that is, Milt?"

"No, Chuck, I surely don't."

"It's because back then, in the fifties, people believed in the American dream, man, you know?"

"See your point..."

"I mean, maybe it wasn't alive back then either. How could it be with fuckin' McCarthy and the HUAC? But people believed it then, man. Now they don't. But they wanna. So they watch this fuckin' crap about the fifties and wish they could go back in time. Back when you could believe in the American dream. 'Cause if you don't believe...then, fuck, what's the use of anything?"

I thought for a minute there Chuck was going to start crying. The thought made my blood run cold. But I just nodded my head.

"So what you gonna do about this, Milt?"

"'Bout the American dream, Chuck?"

"'Bout who killed Henry, Milt."

"Oh. I dunno, Chuck. Tell you the truth, I don't know enough about Jewel and Henry to know who else coulda done it."

Chuck shrugged. "Coulda been a jealous boyfriend or husband or something."

I stared at him through my beer fog. "Huh?"

Chuck laughed. "That Henry was a fuckin' rounder, as my daddy used to say."

"Henry Hotchkiss?"

"Yeah." Chuck shook his head. "Never could understand it. But the women loved him."

"Henry screwed around on my sister?"

"Well, yeah, I guess you could put it that way. Henry'd fuck anything that'd move, Milt. Didn't you know that?"

And I don't know if it was the beer or true self-righteous indignation, but I got pissed. And then I got sad. Because the best suspect for killing a man with a $500,000 life insurance policy who screwed around on his wife was the wife. And the wife was my baby sister. And it was looking more and more like Jewel probably did it. Clean house or no clean house.

"You know this for a fact, Chuck?"

"Oh, yea. He used to fix me up sometimes. Can you imagine that, little old Henry Hotchkiss have to fix *me* up?"

"What do you mean? Fix you up? With women?"

"Yeah. And he had some doozies, too."

And I got pissed again. With a woman like Honey at home, here this no-necked jock was needing to get *fixed up* by my sister's husband. And I wondered if possibly I was the only married man, when I was married, in the whole goddamn world who didn't screw around on his wife. And I thought maybe I should call Mr. Guinness and see if he wanted to put me in his book. Maybe I could go on the talk show circuit, exchange smart cracks with Johnny, and be a punch line for Letterman. I swear to God, sometimes my own sex makes me so goddamn mad I could spit.

Before we got much further, Honey and the kids came home, the kids showing off their new purchases Honey wouldn't let me pay for. I was grateful for that. Money was going to be a problem. I had to send almost half my check back home to cover my house note and utilities and such, which Glenda Sue was handling for me. How in the hell I was going to support three kids and another household on my piddling salary, I didn't know.

And it was on my mind a lot. But not as much as the notion that Henry Hotchkiss, myopic, skinny, bald, short, dull Henry Hotchkiss was a lady-killing asshole.

There was one way to find out if Jewel knew about Henry's extracurricular activities. And that was to ask Honey. But in asking Honey, would I be betraying Chuck and the male bonding we'd just gone through? I never was much on male bonding and I was beginning not to like Chuck very much, but still and all. Maybe I'd ask Chuck what he wanted to do about it.

Honey and the kids went back to the bedrooms to put away their purchases and I asked Chuck about asking Honey whether or not Jewel knew.

"Whether or not Jewel knew what?" he asked.

I sighed. "If Jewel knew Henry was screwing around on her?"

"Oh." He squirmed a little in his chair. "Well, Only problem, Milt, is that, you know, fuck, if we ask Honey that, maybe she's gonna wonder how I knew? And she'd have my dick for dinner if she knew what I did when I was supposed to be bowling." And then he laughed like the idiot he was.

"How 'bout we just ask her if Henry messed around?"

He smiled. "Yeah. We don't know a fuckin' thing, right?" And here he winked at me like the conspirator I was.

After the kids got to bed and Honey settled down in the den with Chuck and I, I asked her.

"Henry? Mess around on Jewel Anne?" She hooted with laughter. "I'm sure the man had balls, but they couldn't a been big enough to do something like that. She'd of fried 'em for breakfast."

And here Chuck looked at me and took a quick gulp of beer to keep from laughing or crying or trembling with fear, whichever.

"So Jewel never said anything about him doing anything like that?" I asked all innocent-like.

"No. Because he never did! She'd have told me. Just like I'd tell her if Chuck did. Right after I killed him." Chuck coughed and spit a little beer onto the coffee table in front of him.

So, I thought, Jewel found out. And she shot him. Just like Honey would do if she found out about Chuck. Just like my wife woulda done if I'd done something that stupid. Naw, the wife woulda just divorced me like she did for my sin of doing nothing more than being boring. And so would Honey probably. And so would Jewel. Women didn't kill their men much for that anymore. Well, some women did. But most didn't. But what about my sister? Did she? Shit, it was beginning to drive me a little crazy.

So maybe I should look into Henry's latest girl-friend. Maybe she was the type to kill. Maybe Henry said he'd divorce Jewel as a way to get in this current lady's pants and then reneged, and she shot him for it. Made sense. Or maybe he was messing with a married lady, like Chuck suggested, and her husband didn't like it. But then why shoot Jewel? Why not wait till Henry was alone? Why would anyone else shoot Jewel? None of it made any sense. The only thing that made sense was that Jewel killed Henry and then tried to kill herself. That's the only thing that made sense. Like it or not. But somewhere in me, I knew. Just like Honey Lancaster knew. Jewel didn't do it. She just didn't do it.

FOUR

ON THE MONDAY of my third week in Houston, Henry's tombstone was finished. The kids were in school, Chuck was at work, and Honey was at the hospital, reading to Jewel from *I'm Okay, You're Okay* and working hard on the child within the woman, or some such. So I went with the men from the monument company to make sure they placed the tombstone on the right grave. I didn't go with 'em when they placed Mama's, and a week later, when I went to visit, I found Mama's tombstone over the grave of Mr. Ralph Littlejohn who'd died in 1934 without benefit of marble marker. So this time, I wasn't taking chances.

And when we got there, there was this lady sitting on the ground by Henry's grave, crying her eyes out. A lady I recognized. From the funeral. Henry's secretary. Well, that made sense.

Her name was Debbie Meeker and she was twenty-six years old. And she wasn't half as pretty as my sister.

When she saw me coming with the workmen, she tried to get up and run, but I got to her before she could.

"Ms. Meeker, right?" I asked, all smiles.

She sniffled. "Yes. You're Mr. Kovak, right? Mrs. Hotchkiss's brother?"

"Yeah. How you doing, Ms. Meeker?"

She sniffled again and tried to smile. Her teeth looked like a model's in a toothpaste commercial. "Oh, I'm just fine, Mr. Kovak. How are you?"

Well, we went on like that for a few minutes while we watched the workmen place the stone. Looking at Henry's name chiseled in marble brought a sob out of little ole Debbie Meeker.

After the workmen had finished and were on their way, I asked the lady, "Did my sister know about you and Henry?"

She just looked straight down at the grave, never taking her eyes off it. "No. Nobody knew. We were very discreet."

"Was he gonna divorce her?"

Finally, she looked at me. "No. Henry was upfront about that from the start. He told me right off the bat that he would never divorce his wife. He also told me I wasn't the only woman in his life, other than his wife. Henry..." she sobbed. "Henry was quite a man, Mr. Kovak. The most incredible lover I've ever had."

Henry? Henry Hotchkiss? I cleared my throat for no reason other than something to do. She went on. "One woman just wasn't enough for Henry. He could make love from dawn to dawn and not get tired. That's why he needed so many different women. He didn't want to wear anybody out."

Well, you gotta hand it to old Henry. He was a right thoughtful asshole.

"You know any of Henry's other women?" I asked.

She thought a moment. "You mean now?"

"Well, whenever?"

"Well, I guess he's been with everybody at work. At least the single women. Henry never dated married women if he could help it."

Henry. What a guy, you know?

"But now," she continued, "I'm just not sure. I've been seeing Henry off and on for a year. Which is how long I was working for him. And I know he was seeing Barbara Almon in payroll for a while but then Barbara got engaged. But I know he used to hang out at a place called After Hours. You might check there. Why do you want to know, anyway?"

"I'm trying to find out who killed him."

"Oh." She looked thoughtful for a minute then said, "I suppose, being Mrs. Hotchkiss's brother and all, you don't want to think she did it. And really, well... I just couldn't see her doing it either. A woman would only do that if she, you know, had a passion for a man. And Mrs. Hotchkiss, well, she just didn't care, you know what I mean?"

"No. I don't, Ms. Meeker. What do you mean?"

"Well, Mrs. Hotchkiss... I guess you could say she could take him or leave him. Henry, I mean. But God, did he love her." She looked at me skeptically and said, "I mean it! He was crazy about her. He'd do anything for her. But she... well, you know, she never even called him on the phone. Not in the whole year I worked for him. He'd call her sometimes, but she never called him. Ever. And, well, you know, when I was going with Eddie—he's my old boyfriend before Henry—well, I used to call him two or three times a day. Everybody does that, when you have a passion."

"Well, they'd been married for a while."

Debbie shook her head. "She never had a passion for him, Mr. Kovak. Just things Henry said...she never loved him really. So why would she kill him?"

Why, indeed. But I knew Debbie Meeker was right. Jewel never did love Henry. Not at the beginning, and I guess not ever.

"Maybe she thought he was going to divorce her and she would lose everything?" I suggested.

Debbie smiled. "He'd never divorce her, Mr. Kovak. He had a real passion for the lady, you know what I mean? And if she divorced him, well, Henry would bend over backwards, live under a bridge, before he'd take anything away from his family. They meant everything to him."

"If Jewel didn't do it, Debbie," I asked, "who did?"

She thought for a moment. "Hell if I know. Too weird for someone just off the street, don't you think? I mean, nothing was taken and shooting Mrs. Hotchkiss to make it look like a suicide, well that's just not what your usual serial killer does, is it?"

"Generally, no," I said.

She sniffled again and looked down at Henry's tombstone. "That's a real nice stone, Mr. Kovak. Henry would've liked that." She shuddered a moment and then looked up at me. "It's hard to believe he's dead, ya know?"

"Yeah, I know," I said, though I didn't really. For some perverse reason, Henry was more real to me now that he was dead than he'd ever been alive.

She held out her hand to me and I shook it. She smiled. "If I can do anything for you, Mr. Kovak, let me know. But I've gotta get back to work. I'm on my lunch hour."

"They find a replacement for Henry yet?"

She shook her head. "No. I'm working in the pool right now. Until somebody decides something. God, I hate it!" She laughed self-consciously, waved, and left, leaving me to stand over my brother-in-law's grave and to wonder just what the hell kind of life he and my sister had had. He loved her and screwed everything in sight. She didn't love him but was faithful. Nothing made any sense anymore. Leastwise, marriage didn't. I guess I always believed in the fairy tales, you know, the ones that ended, ". . . and they lived happily ever after."

But when I got to thinking about the marriages I knew about, Glenda Sue and Lin, where he got his jollies beating the dog shit out of her, Jewel and Henry, with him tomcatting around like it was the right thing to do, Honey and Chuck, with him screwing around and scared to death of her, then think of my own marriage where absolutely nothing untoward happened, no excessive drinking, no gambling, neither of us (to my knowledge) screwing around on the other, neither beating up on the other, and still it ended in divorce, it made you stop and think. And come to no conclusions whatsoever.

When I got back to Jewel's house, I noticed Honey's car in her driveway, so I went next door. Honey smiled that great smile and led me into her living room.

"Jewel's about the same but I swear to God, I think I saw her smile a little today."

I nodded. Honey was always saying that so it didn't mean anything. Every day she saw Jewel frown, smile, grimace, move a toe, something. Nobody else saw it, but Honey did.

"I ran into Henry's secretary at the cemetery today," I told her. And then I told her everything the secretary had told me. Now it could come out, now that Chuck wasn't involved in my having the knowledge.

Her eyes got wide. "You're shitting me! Henry Hotchkiss?" She hooted. "Henry Hotchkiss?" she repeated. "A womanizer? Henry?"

She started laughing and kept at it for quite a while. Finally, finding a tissue and blotting her eyes she said, "The secretary's lying, Milton, that's all it can be! Can you see Henry? I couldn't even visualize him doing it with Jewel, much less every woman..." and she started laughing again. "Henry?"

I didn't share in her laughter so finally she stopped. "She told me about a place where he used to hang out. I'm going by there this evening to see what I can see," I told her. "Would you keep an eye on the kids?"

She shook her head. "No way. I'll have Chuck do it. I'm going with you."

I shook my head. "No way. What would Chuck think?"

Her eyes got wide again. "What? You're worried Chuck will think you and I..."

Then I realized how ludicrous it sounded and felt like a fool. "'Course not. Sure, you can go with me."

"Milton, I didn't mean that that was a stupid idea, or anything, I mean..."

I smiled. "It *was* a stupid idea. Don't worry about it."

When the kids came home, I heated up a casserole one of the neighbor ladies had delivered and fixed a salad to go with it. I swear to God, the women in Houston, at least the ones I'd met so far, were the worst cooks I'd ever come across. Back home, the women of Longbranch wouldn't have slopped the hogs with the concoctions we had for dinner. Everything was covered with Velveeta. Everything. Including the desserts. I swear to God. But the kids ate it like it was good, which is what being a kid is all about, I suppose. And I had to wonder—if my sister's cooking was anything like Mama's, this stuff might seem actually good to them.

Around eight o'clock, Chuck and Honey came over, Chuck to stay with the kids, Honey to go with me. Before we left, though, Chuck pulled me aside.

"Look, I'm not real fuckin' crazy about Honey going to After Hours, ya know?"

"Why's that, Chuck?"

"Well, 'cause I know a couple of ladies there, ya know? And, fuck, what if they said something? Jesus."

I thought about if for a moment. "Well, Chuck, I don't know what I should do about this. If I tell Honey now that she can't go, she'll just go anyway."

Chuck nodded his head, obviously in great fear. "Yeah. Fuck."

"Yeah," I said, and left to join Honey at the door to leave on our mission.

Back home we only have one bar, the Side-winder, which is a pretty sleazy joint full of red-necks looking for fights. We had a murder there just last year. It's not the kind of place you'd take a lady and I was a little worried about taking Honey into After Hours, but I needn't have been. It was a real nice place, with plants and dark wood, leather-covered stools, banquettes also covered in leather, and people dressed like they just came from the of-fice where they did nothing heavier than push a piece of paper from one pile to another. But it took only a few seconds to realize that the people that were grouped together, the men and women, hadn't come in together. I finally made it. After all these years. I was in a singles' bar. Finally. And I have to show up with a woman on my arm. Milton Kovak, sophisticate.

We went straight to the bar where a man of about my age stood, wiping a glass and staring glassy-eyed at his patrons. He had more hair on his upper lip than on the top of his head, but some men are like that. I've noticed over the years that the more hair a man has on his face, underarms, chest and back, the more likely he'll lose it all on top. I have no sci-entific proof of this theory, but just check it out. You'll see I'm right.

I introduced myself as he put down his bar rag to shake my hand.

"Al Taylor," he said, eyeing Honey more than me.

"You usually work nights here?" I asked.

He laughed. "I work nights, days, whenever I'm open. I own the joint."

I showed him a picture of Henry. "You know this guy?" I asked.

Al looked at it for no more than a second or two and said, "Yeah. That's Henry. Hear his wife offed him. Too bad. Gave me a lot of business."

"Can I ask you a few questions about him?"

"You a cop?"

I flashed my badge quickly, just quick enough for him to see it was official, but not long enough to see that I was way out of my jurisdiction.

"What'd you wanna know?" he asked.

"Did you ever see Henry here with a woman?"

Al laughed. "Man, are you serious? Yeah, I saw Henry here with a woman. Every time he came in, he found a woman. Why the fuck else would he come in?"

"The same woman or different women?"

He shrugged. "Sometimes he'd get a repeater. The ladies really liked Henry. I figured he musta had a dong the size of Texas the way they liked him.

Excuse me, ma'am,'' he said to Honey, his voice sarcastic as if he figured she probably liked that kinda talk.

"Are any of Henry's women in here now?" I asked.

Al looked around at his patrons who numbered about twenty on this weekday night. "Yeah. 'Bout half a dozen. The boy got around, I'm telling you.'' He began pointing out women and stopped at what I counted as seven. Seven women in the same bar in one night and they'd all slept with my brother-in-law. If I hadn't been so pissed at Henry, I woulda been in awe, and that's the God's truth.

Of the seven women, four were with men, one was sitting by herself, and two were sitting together. I figured I'd hit the one by herself first, as she'd more than likely be the first to get paired off. The lady was about forty, had dyed red hair, wore her lipstick like she was outlining lips that weren't there, and was a little on the hefty side. Her name was Alice.

After we'd introduced ourselves, Honey and I sat down at her table. Alice kept eyeing Honey, as if not sure how to talk with a man in the presence of another woman. Some women are like that.

"You knew Henry Hotchkiss?"

She shrugged and I showed her the picture.

She shrugged again and then sighed. "Yeah, I knew Henry. What a waste! I can't believe she killed him. The greatest goddamn fuck in the world and his wife shot him!"

She shook her head several times, the dyed hair not moving from all the hairspray. "How long's it been since you were with Henry?" I asked.

She thought for a moment and said, "Guess about a week before he died. On a Wednesday. I met him here during lunch and we went to my place."

No wonder the boy was so skinny, I thought to myself, he never ate.

"You married?" I asked.

She shook her head. "Divorced. Three times." For some reason, she gave the number with a lot of pride in her voice.

"Henry ever talk to you about getting a divorce and you two getting married?"

She laughed. "Henry? Never! He told me up front on the first night I met him that he was married and loved his wife and would never divorce her. I mean, the first night I met him! I almost didn't go out with him, but...well, there was something about Henry..."

And that's what they all said. All seven of them, when I got them alone and questioned them.

"There was something about Henry..." All seven of the women there tonight were divorced ladies, with the exception of one woman in her thirties who had an open marriage. She pointed at a man three tables over with his tongue down the throat of a sweet young thing and said that was her husband. When I'd asked to talk with her, the lady herself had her hand on the leg of her table companion. And this was Houston. I wondered what in the hell went on in places like Los Angeles and New York.

After interviewing all the ladies, Honey and I got a table to ourselves and signaled to Al for two beers.

"Henry?" Honey was still not sure the ladies were talking about her next-door neighbor. And then she got indignant. "If he screwed anything that moved, how come he never propositioned me? What am I, oatmeal?"

I smiled. "No, you certainly aren't that. I figure he left you alone because you lived next door and were Jewel's best friend."

She sighed. "Yeah, that must be it, huh?"

"The only reason I can think of," I said and could feel myself blushing.

Honey put her head in her hand and looked up at me with those shiny, light brown eyes. "Are you flirting with me, Milton Kovak?"

I toyed with my beer a moment, not able not to stop myself from thinking about the last time I flirted with a married lady. "A little bit, I guess," I said, adding, "but it doesn't mean much."

"What does that mean, 'It doesn't mean much'?"

I shrugged. "You're a married lady."

"And if I wasn't?"

I grinned. "You'd be in big trouble."

She grinned back. "Good. I'm glad to hear that."

The waitress brought us our beers and I showed her Henry's picture. Of all the women in the room, with the exception of Honey, that waitress was the prettiest. In her mid to late twenties, with rich brown hair falling past her shoulders, she wore her apron with the same kind of dignity I'd noticed in Glenda Sue. In fact, although younger and with darker hair, she reminded me a lot of Glenda Sue.

"He ever get in any trouble around here that you know about? Messing with a married lady, anything like that?"

"Henry? Naw, he'd never do that. Except for Shirley, and everybody messes with Shirley. But her husband gets off to that so no big deal."

"What's your name?" I asked.

"Lisa." She smiled at me and I smiled back. I didn't look at Honey because I figured she wouldn't be smiling. Women are like that. I introduced myself and Honey and told her what I was up to.

"Can you join us a minute or are you real busy?"

She looked around the room and shrugged. "Everybody seems happy right now. Maybe just a minute or two."

She maneuvered her way between Honey and me, which I found flattering as hell. I tried not to think about what Honey thought. After all, Honey was a married lady. And nowadays, I didn't truck with married ladies. It only takes Milton Kovak once of getting shat upon to learn these things. Like they say, I'm a real quick study.

"How about you?" I asked, hoping like hell the answer was no. "You ever go out with Henry?"

She shook her head and I was more pleased than I had any right to be. "Naw. Henry wasn't my type. And I guess I wasn't his. We never hit it off."

Not his type? I thought female was his "type."

"I thought the police said his wife did it?" Lisa said.

"That's what they think," I told her, "but that's not what I think. Or Honey here, who was Henry's wife's best friend. We're pretty sure..."

Honey made a snorting sound. "Pretty sure? I *know* Jewel didn't do it! And you should *know* it too, Milton Kovak!"

For some reason, the two women glared at each other, then Honey glared at me. I did the only thing I knew to do. I chugged my beer.

"Lisa! You working for a living or what?" Al the bartender called.

Lisa stood up and smiled down at me. "I wish I could've been more help, Milt, but..."

I took out one of my cards. Two years ago, the Sheriff had had this whim to buy him and me business cards. I had two hundred of the damn things and in two years I had only given out four of 'em. The Sheriff hadn't even opened his box yet. I scratched Jewel's phone number and address on the back of the card.

"If you think of anything," I said standing up, "please let me know."

She smiled and read both sides of the card slowly. "You bet, Milt. And if you need anything else, well..."

And she walked off real slow and I had a hard time breathing right. And then I looked at Honey and figured if she had her way, I wouldn't be breathing at all.

"You ready to leave?" she said, her voice icy cold.

"Sure," I said, carefully leaving exactly fifteen percent as tip. Less and Lisa wouldn't be so cooperative next time, more and Honey would be able to ice-skate home.

We were silent all the way home and even though I knew why, I wondered about it. Honey had been pretty damn clear about nothing going on between us, I'd been clear about that too. But still she was mad because another woman flirted with me. Or I flirted with another woman. I'm not sure exactly what happened there. And I wasn't exactly sure what was happening here, either.

When we walked in Jewel's front door, Honey made a beeline for the den where Chuck sat and kissed him a passionate hello. I swear to God, women kill me. I could live to be a thousand, and I'll never figure 'em out. But I guess, in its own way, that's good.

Chuck, bless him, was so thankful she was kissing him rather than killing him that he got a little carried away and I thought I might have to leave the two of them alone, but after about half a minute they managed to pull themselves apart.

"You find out anything?" he asked, talking to me but looking at his wife.

"Just that Henry screwed everything that walked," I said.

Chuck looked at me. "Fuck, you already knew that."

I sat down on the couch and sighed. "Yeah. I sure did." I shook my head. "I don't know. All I seem to be finding out here is that my brother-in-law was a womanizer of the enth degree. But not one of his women seemed to want to see him dead." I sighed again. "I don't know where to go from here."

Chuck gave me an affectionate pat on the leg that I was afraid would take a day and a half to heal. "You'll come up with something, Milt. We got faith in you, right, Honey?"

Honey shrugged her pretty shoulders. "Whatever," she said.

FIVE

"MAYBE WE'RE GOING about this all wrong," I said the next day to Honey. She'd forgiven me for the night before, which I figured was mighty nice of her and all, and we were sitting over coffee and sweet rolls in Jewel's used-to-be clean kitchen.

"How do you mean?" she asked, a dollop of jelly sticking to the corner of her mouth as she bit into her roll. I had this overwhelming urge to lick off that jelly, but I restrained myself. That's the kinda fella I am.

"I mean," I said, staring hard at the dollop of jelly, "maybe this hasn't got anything to do with Henry's women."

"Then what else could it be? You're not gonna start this shit about Jewel again are you?"

I held up my hand to ward off any blows and denied what she said. "Of course not. I mean, what else was there in Henry's life besides his family and his women?"

She shrugged a shoulder and her tongue came out and flicked daintily at the dollop of jelly. I sighed.

"His work," I said. "He was an accountant, right?"

"For an oil company, not the Mafia."

"Still and all..."

She put down her sweet roll and took a sip of coffee, and then shook her head. "Gotta be the women, Milt."

"No. Now wait a minute. What was the name of the company Henry worked for?"

"TPD Oil Industries."

"Oil drilling, exploration, what?"

"Yep. Drilling, exploration, supplies, you name it. They did it."

"Real big company?"

"No. Not that big. Not Exxon- or Texaco-big. Actually, midsize, I guess."

"When most of the midsize companies got their presidents in the unemployment lines, right?"

"Well, yeah, a lot of 'em went under. TPD was lucky, I guess."

"Uh-huh," I said.

"What does that mean? Uh-huh?"

"I think I'd like to know a little bit more about that outfit, that's all," I said.

"Why?"

I shrugged. "Henry didn't mess around with married women. No jealous husbands. Nothing is missing from the house. No burglar. Jewel didn't do it. There are two basic reasons why somebody murders—sex and money. If we rule out the sex angle, which I can't figure out how not to at this point anyway, that leaves money. Money was Henry's business. He was an accountant. Let's say he found out something about TPD. Something not quite kosher. As their accountant, he'd have access to their books. If he was a good accountant, maybe he figured out something he shouldn't have. So they silenced him.''

Honey giggled. ''Milt, you been reading too many mystery stories.''

I'll admit my feelings were a little ruffled. ''So you got any bright ideas, lady?''

''One of his bimbos killed him.''

''Which one and why?''

''Hell, I don't know which one.''

''Why? Why'd she do it?''

''Because he wouldn't marry her.''

''Dumb.''

The honey-colored eyes started blazing away at me. ''As dumb as your theory of a great big oil conspiracy.''

''Well, I'm the professional here and that's the only theory I got at the moment.'' I reached over to the phone on the wall and took down the receiver which had the dialing apparatus in the handle. "What's the number for TPD?"

"How would I know? I never called Henry. Unless of course, we were having a secret affair and *I* killed him because he wouldn't marry me! Or," and here she started grinning real big, "I killed him because he wanted to marry me and I was afraid he'd tell Chuck. How's that?"

"Get the goddamn phone book and look up Deborah Meeker."

She wasn't listed. "Then look up TPD."

She blandly sipped her coffee. "Ever hear of information? Do it yourself, Detective."

"You think Jewel can afford an extra twenty cents on her phone bill?"

She got up and went to a drawer, pulled it out and extracted the Houston business pages. "You know, Kovak, you're a real pain in the ass."

"You know, Lancaster, so are you. But you're cute."

She threw the book at me. "Cute! Cute? Why don't you just pat me on the head and say, 'Nice puppy'?"

I riffled the pages back to the T's and found the number. "So what's wrong with 'cute'? Cute's a nice word. You are cute."

She sat down at the table and nibbled at her last little piece of sweet roll. "I don't want to be cute," she said, her face in a frown. "I want to be svelte, mysterious, gorgeous, beautiful, striking. Any adjective in the world except cute!"

Dialing TPD's number, I said, "Lady, I'm not gonna play the adjective game with you. Your husband's too big for that."

She smiled. I smiled and somebody answered the phone. "Debbie Meeker, please," I said in my best deputy-doing-business voice.

"Ms. Meeker is no longer employed by TPD," said the smiley-sounding voice on the other end.

"Oh, really? Since when?"

"I'm not allowed to give out that information, sir. Would you like to speak to our personnel office?"

"Yeah, I'd like that a whole bunch."

I waited while she switched me over, listening to a Montovani-style rendition of "Honky-Tonk Woman" that came over the wire while I waited. Finally a nice lady voice came on the line. "Perkins, Personnel. May I help you?"

"Yes, ma'am. I hope so. I'm looking for Debbie Meeker. The lady that answered the phone first says she's not there anymore. Can you tell me when she quit?"

"Officially, her termination date was as of yesterday, but we haven't seen Ms. Meeker since February seventeenth."

I looked at the calendar hanging on the wall in Jewel's kitchen. February 17 had been the day Henry's monument had been installed. The day I talked to Debbie Meeker at the cemetery. "What do you mean, Ms. Perkins? You haven't seen her?"

"According to her supervisor, she left for lunch on Monday and has not yet returned. Under the circumstances, we had no choice but to terminate her employment."

"You checked her house? See if she was okay?"

"That would have been up to her supervisor, sir. Not me."

"Can I speak to the supervisor?"

"May I ask your name, sir?"

"Joe Meeker. Debbie's my daughter."

Honey's eyebrow shot up and I grinned.

"Certainly, Mr. Meeker. I'll transfer you to the supervisor. His name is James Sonfield. Good luck, Mr. Meeker."

I thanked her and listened to the tail end of "Honky-Tonk Woman" and the beginning of "Moon River" done on a zither before James Sonfield picked up the line. Obviously, Ms. Perkins had told Mr. Sonfield what was going on.

"Mr. Meeker, this is James Sonfield. I understand you're looking for Debbie?"

"That's right, Mr. Sonfield. Ms. Perkins said she left on the seventeenth for lunch and you haven't seen her since?"

"That's right, sir."

"Did you call her apartment?"

"Well, no sir, I didn't. We have quite a turn-around in personnel here, and it didn't seem worth the effort. Have you called?"

Now this is where it was going to get tricky. "Son, I can't," I said in my most fatherly voice. "She moved a while back and my wife took down the new number but now we can't find it. Her grandma's real sick, in the hospital, and we need to get ahold of her."

"Just a minute, Mr. Meeker, let me see if I have her number."

I got to listen to the zither rendition of "Moon River" some more before Sonfield came back on the line. And I'll be damned if he didn't just up and give me the number. Pretty as you please. I thanked him, hung up, and dialed Debbie Meeker's number. And got a recording saying the number was no longer in service.

"Now that's real strange," I said to Honey. "Wish I knew where she lived. I'd go over there and have a look."

"So let's find out."

"How?"

"The city directory. They cross-reference by name, address, and *telephone number!*"

"No shit?"

She grinned. "No shit, Sherlock." She got up and slipped on her shoes that had been sitting under the table. She had real pretty feet. I'd noticed that. Right off the bat. "So let's go."

I got up and put on my jacket. "Where to? You got one of them? A city directory?"

"No, but Chuck does. At his office."

So we got in Honey's car and drove to the little strip shopping center where Chuck had his office. Except for Chuck, a U-Totum, and a submarine sandwich shop, the center was empty, with about four storefronts with FOR LEASE signs on them.

Chuck was on the phone when we walked in. There was a secretary at a desk at the front of the office, a lady of about sixty, with white hair and grandmotherly ways. I figured Honey had something to do with the hiring of her. She was busy at the typewriter when we walked in but looked up, saw us, stopped her typing, and grinned real big at Honey.

"Hi, darlin'," she called. "How are you?"

"Hi, Mom. I'm fine. Need to talk to what's-his-name."

The woman looked behind her. "Who? That big old lummox? Why would anybody want to talk with him?"

They both laughed and Honey introduced me to what turned about to be Chuck's mother, Lucille Lancaster.

Chuck got off the phone and walked into the area where we stood with his mother. "Hey, babe," he said, leaning way down to kiss his wife on the cheek.

"We need to see your city directory. The defective detective here thinks he has a lead," Honey said, pointing at me.

"No fuck? That's great!" He went back to his part of the office and came back with a huge book, about four times the size of the business pages I'd been playing with earlier.

"The problem's gonna be," Honey said, "how long she's had that number. This book only comes out, what, every two years or so?" She looked at Chuck for confirmation.

He shrugged. "Something like that."

But we were in luck. In comparing the phone number I'd written down with the numbers in the book, we found one on a street called Fountainview listed under the name of D. B. Meeker. But Honey didn't seem to be too pleased.

"Oh, great," she said. "No apartment number listed."

"So?" I said, all innocent-like.

"So Fountainview is a street about three or four blocks long with one giant apartment complex on it. It could take a month."

"Unless we find a manager willing to talk."

Honey grinned. "That should be no problem for you, Mr. Meeker."

We drove in toward the city and found the street with no problem since Honey knew exactly where she was going. And she had been right. It was a massive apartment complex with apartments all along the street front and more going back at least another city block. And somewhere in all this was Debbie Meeker. Or where she used to be anyway.

We went to the management office and were in luck. The little girl at the desk, barely over eighteen, had only been working there a week and was happy as a clam to give out a resident's apartment number. And she even gave us a little map showing us exactly where to go. And I didn't even tell her I was the resident's father. I hoped like hell her boss would soon inform her that that wasn't the way to do business.

Debbie Meeker's apartment was in Unit C, on the second floor facing one of the many pools the complex boasted. I figured if Longbranch had had a place like this, I'da been in hog heaven. Apartment 217 was Debbie's and there was no answer to our knock. But when I tried the doorknob, the door opened in my hand.

But being a police officer, knowing the restrictions thereof, I didn't move.

Honey nudged me. "Go on in," she said in a stage whisper.

"That's breaking and entering," I said.

"Not breaking," she giggled. "Just entering."

She was right. I opened the door a little further and looked in. To see an empty apartment. Obviously, Debbie Meeker had neglected to inform the management that she no longer lived there. It was a nice one-bedroom with stained, off-white carpet, a fake fireplace, a big living room. We searched all the cupboards and closets and found absolutely nothing. Not even any trash.

When I came out from my futile search of the bedroom and bathroom, Honey was sitting on the little brick hearth by the fake fireplace.

"Now what, Hercule?" she asked.

"Hell if I know," I said, sitting down beside her. "Seems kinda funny, is all."

"What seems funny?"

"Her taking off like that. Right after I talked with her. Didn't even go back to work. Why do you suppose she did that?"

Honey shrugged then grinned. "I know," she said. "Somebody was at the cemetery and saw her talking to you. So they kidnapped her and probably killed her. Then came back here and cleaned out her apartment to make it look like she skipped town."

I glared at her which just made her grin all the harder. "You're a real funny lady. Excuse me while I bust a gut laughing."

"You know what your problem is, Milton?" she asked.

"No, Honey, what's my problem?"

She stood up and walked toward the door. "You got no sense of humor."

SIX

THE NEXT MORNING, while the kids were eating breakfast, Carl informed me that he was supposed to be a tree in a school play that started in two days and what could I do about a costume? And I just looked at him like he was the crazy little kid he was.

"Jeez, is that all they do at that damn school?" Leonard said. "Make you dress up like trees? They made me do that when I was a kid, too."

"So what'd you do for a costume?" I asked.

"Mama made one," Marlene said. "It's probably up in the attic if you don't feel like making another one, Uncle Milt."

And I had this little warm feeling all over. This was the first time since I'd come to Houston that any of the kids had called me "Uncle Milt." I liked it. They usually didn't address me at all. And I also liked the fact that I didn't have to figure out what to do about a costume.

"Well, I'll go up in the attic today and see if I can find it. Carl, that be okay by you?"

He shrugged. "Sure. Mama woulda made me a new one, but..."

He shrugged again and the other kids looked down at their plates. Have I mentioned what great kids my little sister has? Maybe all kids are like them, I don't know, but these kids...I knew they were hurting, and it would come out sometimes in little ways, weird little silences at weird times, going off to their rooms when it got to them, but mostly it was business as usual. Leonard was the one I worried about the most, though. He hadn't really talked to me much since his fight at school that first day, and I wondered if killing was still on his mind. But I didn't know how to bring it up. "Say, Leonard, you still thinking about murdering somebody?" just didn't seem right somehow.

But other than that one little scene with Leonard, things went pretty smoothly. The kids kept up each other's spirits and they worked, God, did they work. It wasn't like the way it would have been at my mama's house either, where the girl child would have been the one to get the burden of the housework.

Jewel and Henry had done their job, that's for sure. The boys took turns doing the laundry and running the vacuum cleaner, just as much as Marlene. I was impressed. After the wife left me, I had to get a neighbor lady over to the house to teach me how to turn on the washing machine. But that was a long time ago. Now I can wash almost a whole load without changing the colors of the clothes.

After the kids had gone to school, I went up to the attic in search of the tree costume. The entrance was in the bedroom hallway and it was one of those trap doors with a rope hanging off it where you pull on it and it's got folding stairs you pull down. So I did all that and went up the stairs.

The attic was as neat as the rest of the house. There were a lot of boxes, but they were all neatly labeled and all arranged around the little standing platform so you didn't have to worry about falling through the ceiling to get to anything. Also up there was an old baby bed and the cradle. I saw the cradle and didn't gasp with surprise, being a man with total control of my emotions like I am. I didn't know what had happened to it. I thought it was long gone and hadn't even missed it when Jewel and I had cleaned out Mama's house after her death.

But I guessed Mama had probably sent it to Jewel when her first baby was on the way. That's the kind of thing Mama would do.

Daddy and I had built that cradle. It was the first time I'd actually done any real work with Daddy. Up until then, I'd just been there to hand him a tool and to bounce cuss words off of. But that had been our first real project together. I'd drawn up the plans all by myself and together we'd bought the wood, good oak, and cut the pieces and put them together with wooden pegs rather than nails because it looked cleaner and lasted longer. And we'd painted it, using a stencil we'd bought at the hardware store to put an outline of a teddy bear on both ends.

We'd finished it two weeks before Jewel was born. Mama didn't know what we were doing out there in the garage every night. It was our surprise for her and the baby. She'd cried when we brought it in and presented it to her. And she kissed us both and told me I was going to be the best big brother in the world.

The yellow paint on the cradle was faded now and peeling in places and the teddy bears, pink on one end, blue on the other, were almost gone. I reached across a box to where it sat and pulled it to me. It was dusty and had lost one of the wooden pegs so that one side was a little loose. And I held that cradle in my arms and began to cry, great heaving sobs that shook my body and the ladder where my feet rested. And I prayed to God that Jewel make it. Because only then could I make up to her all those years. Only if she made it could I fulfill Mama's prophesy and become the best big brother in the world. Well, if not that at this late date, at least one that she could possibly forgive.

After a while, I pulled myself together and found the right box with the costume and dug it out. I took it and the cradle back down stairs and washed the costume out by hand, afraid the washing machine might ruin it. I put it in the dryer on the lowest, gentlest heat, and when it had dried sufficiently, I took it out and ironed every leaf. I may not be a Catholic, but us card-carrying Baptists know about penance too.

When I was through, I hung it as best I could on a hanger and left the house for the nearest hardware store. It took a while to find a stencil that looked anything like the one Daddy and I had used, but I found one eventually. I bought yellow, pink, and blue paint, and a wooden peg. It wasn't as good as the ones Daddy and I had made, but it would do. And I went home and repaired and repainted the cradle.

By early afternoon, it was dry and I took it to the hospital with me. Standing in the doorway of the Intensive Care Unit, I looked at my baby sister lying there on her back, with tubes running every which way and the earphones in her ears teaching her Spanish. I put down the cradle and sat gingerly on the bed, carefully removing the earphones from her ears and placing them on the bedside table, turning off the tape recorder while I was about it. I took one of her hands in mine and stroked it.

"Jewel, I'm sorry. I'm so sorry," I said, tears running down my face, "I did something to you a long time ago I never should have done. I pretended that you didn't exist. I shut you out of my life. And when you needed me, I bounced into your life acting like I had some authority over it. Over you. All I can say, Jewel, is that if I had it to do all over again, I'd do it different. I swear to you I would."

I picked up the cradle and propped one end on the bed, resting her hand on it. "I made this for you, me and Daddy, before you were ever born. It was so important to me then. You were so important. I don't know why I shut you out after you were born. Jealousy, I guess. But I'm paying for it now, Jewel, if that's any help. I'm all alone in this world. You and your kids are my only kin, and I've shut you out for so long, I don't know if you'll let me let you in. Or if you even wanna be. But you gotta come out of this coma, Jewel. Before it's too late. You've gotta do it soon. If for nothing other than to tell me to go fuck myself. And you gotta do it for those kids of yours. They need you so goddamn much. They're great kids, Jewel, you've done a terrific job. But your job's not finished. They can't make it with just me. They gotta have you. So come on back, Jewel, please. And do it quick, honey...."

A sob caught in my throat and I felt an arm around my shoulder. I looked up to see Honey standing there beside me. She put my head against her breast and held me with her arms around my back and I cried long and hard.

Finally, she led me away from the bed and took the cradle and put it next to the nightstand by the bed. Taking my hand, she led me out of the ICU.

"If that doesn't do it, Milton, nothing will." She smiled up at me and reached up a hand to touch my cheek. "She'd be damn stupid to die now."

That night, around midnight, I got a call from Dr. Hussain. Through the heavy accent, I discovered he was telling me that my sister had come out of the coma. No one knows for sure what's going on with a person when they're in a coma. Whether part of them is awake, seeing and hearing what's going on, or if they're just in this limbo state they either come out of or they don't. At least, the doctors don't know it or won't tell it. But I knew. I wouldn't have been one bit surprised if Jewel sat up and started talking Spanish to one and all.

After I got the call, I called Honey and woke her up and told her, and she and Chuck came over to the house, him staying with the kids while Honey and I drove through the dark and semi-deserted streets to the hospital. The nurses didn't want to let us in, but then Dr. Hussain came up and said yes. Do it. It may not have been the words, because who could understand them? But the authority was there, and they let us in.

She looked just like she'd looked when I last saw her, tubes running in and out of her, the eyelids closed over the sparkling emerald eyes. I looked at Dr. Hussain and he smiled and reached out and gently touched her, saying something only he understood.

Slowly, the eyelids lifted and the green eyes looked up at the doctor and slowly moved to where Honey and I stood. A smile played across the dried and cracked lips, and her tongue came out to slowly moisten them. In a voice I didn't recognize, she said, "Hi, Honey." She looked at me and frowned for a moment then smiled slowly. "Don't I know you from somewhere?" she said.

"This is your brother, Milton..." Honey started, but Jewel lifted a hand weakly to stop her.

"It...was a...joke, Honey," she said.

And Honey burst into tears and threw her arms around Jewel's neck. Jewel grimaced in pain and the doctor pulled Honey off her friend, telling her in no uncertain terms, which we determined only by his manner not his words, not to do that again.

"What time is it?" Jewel asked.

"After midnight," I told her.

"What time did they bring me in here?"

Honey and I looked at each other, then at the doctor. We got the impression now was not the time to tell her she'd been in a coma almost a month.

"Little while ago," I lied.

"Where's Henry?" she asked.

The doctor took that one, telling her, I think, that now was the time to get some sleep. Honey and I took turns kissing her good-bye and we left, holding hands all the way out to the car.

In the car, Honey put her arms around me and cried and I'm ashamed to admit that I wasn't thinking about Jewel a lot at that moment. It had been a while and that round little body felt too good as I held her.

Finally, she stopped crying and looked into my eyes. "You did it, Milt," she said, smiling at me. "You brought her out of it."

I shook my head. "Won't be what the doctors say."

"Screw doctors. They don't know diddly." She stroked my cheek and I felt myself coming alive and willed it to go away.

I took her hand and held it away from my face. "You ought not to do that, Honey," I said quietly.

And then she kissed me. And it was long and hard and hot and I held on to her so hard I was afraid she might break.

Pulling away from her, I said, "The dumbest thing in the world for us to do would be finish this."

She leaned her head against the headrest and said, "Yeah. You're right." She looked at me and smiled. "I've been married to Chuck for fourteen years. I met him when he was playing for LSU. I was a cheerleader. That was seventeen years ago. Since the day I met him, I've never looked at another man. Never wanted another man. I guess just wanting you is enough of a sin, huh?"

And I started to say something about if it was already a sin, we might as well . . . but I didn't. I just said, "Chuck's a damned lucky man." And we drove on back to Jewel's house.

THE NEXT MORNING, I told the kids before breakfast that their Mama was out of the coma. And the boys did something that I could blackmail them with the rest of their lives if I was that kind of an uncle, which I'm proud to say I'm not. They burst into tears and all three hugged each other, then me. When I could break away, I called the two schools the three attended and told them that the kids would be in late that day and told them why. I could sense the smiles through the phone and heard the wishes of good luck.

My sister was alive and conscious and on her way to recovery. All I had left to do was prove that she didn't kill her husband and shoot herself. Just that little bitty old thing.

The kids, when we got to the hospital, were so gentle with their mother you'd think she'd break, which she probably might have done. They had strict orders from me: don't mention Henry. Don't mention the day of the week or the week of the month. Just mention how much they love her. That's all she needs to hear, I said.

The kids cried and Jewel cried and I cried and even the nurse had a tear in her eye. But we had to leave after only fifteen minutes, with promises of being back the next time the doors opened. I stopped on my way out to talk to Dr. Hussain, taking the little nurse who had interpreted the first time with me. I asked him when I could question my sister about the shooting and if the police had asked the same question or if they knew she was out of her coma. They knew, because Dr. Hussain had to tell them, which he did first thing that morning. But they weren't all that anxious, according to him, to question her. I guess they figured they already had their answers. Damn 'em.

He told me that later that day, as her strength was returning so rapidly, he and I together would talk to her, letting her know how long she'd been in the hospital and what had happened to Henry.

After I'd dropped the kids off at school and got back to Jewel's house, I walked over to Honey's and asked her if she'd go with me to the hospital.

She seemed a little awkward at first, unable to look me in the eye.

"Of course. I'll do anything for Jewel, you know that," she said. Looking out at her winter-dead lawn, three inches to my left.

"Honey..." She adjusted her eyes, this time looking to my right at an evergreen. I put my hand to her face and gently moved her head toward me. That made her look right at me.

"Last night was my fault," I said, "and it will never happen again. I know you're a happily married lady who was very vulnerable because of her best friend's condition. I took advantage of that and I'm sorry."

A smile played across her lips and then she burst out laughing.

"That's the damnedest thing I've ever heard!" she said between fits of laughter. "Big gallant man takes all the blame on his big he-man shoulders! Milton, you slay me!"

I shrugged. "Well, I was only trying..."

She put a finger to my lips and followed it with a quick kiss, her lips barely touching mine. "I know what you were trying to do, Milton," she said, "absolve me of all guilt. But if I remember correctly, I'm the one who kissed you..."

"But only because..."

"And I enjoyed the hell out of it!" She stopped smiling and said, "But you're right. It won't happen again. Even if I want it to."

I sighed. "Lady, you're not making this easy."

"I guess me wanting you and you wanting me is just gonna have to be enough."

I smiled and shook my head. "I just try to keep thinking what Chuck would do to me if he even knew I thought about it..."

She laughed. "Not a pretty picture."

I shuddered. "Downright ugly picture, you wanna know the truth."

We stood there for a few seconds, just smiling at each other in our secret and then I said, "So, I'll pick you up about noon for the next visiting time. That okay?"

"See you then." She shut the door and I walked back to Jewel's house wondering what this fascination was I had with married women. Did I maybe need to see a shrink? With Glenda Sue home in Longbranch waiting patiently for me, feeding my cat and watering my plant and paying my bills, what the hell was I doing in Houston rubbing up on a married lady?

But I couldn't help smiling and thinking to myself that she was something, Honey was, something different and wonderful and just a little bit crazy. Not like Laura, not at all. And maybe it wasn't just married ladies, maybe it was just something about a lady named Honey Lancaster. Or was I just trying to excuse my own craziness?

IT WAS ROUGH. The visit with Jewel. First we told her what day it was and how long she'd been in a coma. She had a hard time with that. With losing almost a month out of her life and the lives of her children.

And then I said, "Jewel, do you know what happened? Why you're in here?"

Her hand went tentatively to her head where the bandages covered her wound and she shook her head gently, a puzzled look on her face. "A car wreck?" She shook her head again. "I don't remember..."

"It was a Friday night," I told her, "the kids went to a basketball game at the high school. You and Henry were alone in the house..."

"No. I had to go to the store. We were out of bread and milk and I had to make a quick stop..."

I smiled encouragingly.

"I had a wreck on my way back?" she asked, looking from me to Honey to the doctor.

"No, Jewel. You got back to the house. Do you remember what happened when you got there?"

She lay in the bed, fighting with her fading memories and I felt for her like I never had before. Finally, she said, "Henry was home, wasn't he?"

"Yes," I said.

"But he wasn't alone. He had a visitor..." She faded away for a moment and closed her eyes. "I think so. I think he had a visitor."

"Who was it, Jewel, who was Henry's visitor?"

She slowly shook her head from side to side. "I don't know," she said, a whine creeping into her voice. "I don't know, just go away, okay? Tell Henry I want to see him when you leave."

The doctor motioned us from the room and we left, congregating in the hall to discuss what had happened.

Honey hit me hard on the shoulder. "I told you! Didn't I tell you? Henry had a visitor! Jewel never shot him and I knew it all the damned time!'' But there was relief in her voice and on her face, just like I knew there was on mine, because knowing it in your heart is one thing, but hearing it with your head is something entirely different.

"... police ... ?" Dr. Hussain said.

"We should tell the police what she said?" I asked.

He nodded his head. "... Mrs ... hoot ... don't ja know?"

"She didn't shoot him?"

He beamed at me and we both nodded our heads at each other and smiled. "Why don't you go ahead and tell the police that, Doctor? Might mean more coming from you."

He smiled and nodded his head up and down and was on his way to find a phone.

SEVEN

DESPITE THE FACT that in many ways, Houston, Texas, is by far the biggest human garbage pit I've ever been in, there's an energy about the city that's infectious. I can only imagine what it must have been like in the fifties, back when oil was gold and oilmen were kings. Back when there was a debutante on every street corner and the booze and money flowed. Back when men tipped parking lot attendants with hundred-dollar bills and women gave dinner parties for five hundred of their closest friends. Back when movie stars came to the city for hotel openings and stayed in drunken stupors for months on end. Back when Houston was boomtown, not bust town.

But even now, with used-to-be engineers selling shoes and has-been geologists pumping gas, not oil, the city has a vitality you can feel. Maybe it was just the last dying shudder of the corpse, but it was there. In its way, Houston is as big a melting pot as New York or Los Angeles. With two major universities and the "awl bidness" that used to be, you could find every nationality known to man. They lived in neighborhoods from Chinatown to the not-so-small enclave of Iranians, from the barrios to the community not far from my sister's house of actual, real, live gypsies. Romanian style.

Defunct strip shopping centers became market places for the different ethnic groups, and in traveling the city, you could close your eyes and a minute later end up in Casablanca, Saigon, or Mexico City. And, as in any city, you could buy anything you wanted if you had the dough-re-me. From piñatas and pita bread to crack and small boys.

But all of this doesn't mean that my fondest wish wasn't to rewrite that old song of Mac Davis's and see Houston in the rearview mirror. Especially after my trip with Chuck to inspect the site of a claim on an insurance policy he'd sold. The company suspected arson and asked Chuck to go take a look before they sent their company man down. Chuck asked me along.

It was on the north side of the real downtown area, close enough to the million-dollar highrises to spit. On a road called Jensen. The road wove through a lower-middle-class area for a while, then ended abruptly in an area uglier than anything I'd seen on TV. Half the buildings were burned out, with people living inside the ruins, little kids running around half naked in the cold.

As we got out of the car, I saw what could only have been a pimp, a black guy in bright colored polyester, a huge green hat with a purple feather, wearing high-heeled boots, taking a swat at a very pregnant lady in stiletto heels and gold lamé. And this was at nine o'clock in the morning. We were approached by two such ladies before we crossed the street.

"Hey, sugah, make you happy, baby..."

"Wanna go round the world wid me, honey...?"

Chuck and I just kept walking.

"I see what you mean about your town, Chuck," I said, as we reached the building he was to inspect. "Things are bad."

He shook his head. "This area was like this in the heyday. Every city's got one, good times and bad times, I suppose. Man, sometimes, I look at these people, and I wanna bust something. Or bust out crying. Fuck, I dunno."

We were quiet the rest of the time, with me thinking only of Longbranch, Oklahoma. Yeah, we had poor people, probably more than our share since the economy got bad, but not like this. I'm not sure what the difference was, but they weren't like this. Maybe it had something to do with hope. Or maybe I'm just full of shit. Won't be the first time. But all in all, that little trip just assured me I wanted to go home.

I'd only been in my new house up on Mountain Falls Road for a couple of months. And I missed it. That's nuts, right? Missing a house? But it's true. I've never been a man big on possessions, probably because I never had any that were really mine.

When I was a kid, everything I had belonged to my parents, with the exception possibly of my baseball card collection and my '55 Chevy, bought and paid for from the proceeds of three summers bagging at the A & P. They let me take that and the cards with me when I moved on.

While I was married, although my money actually bought everything we had, house, car, furniture, all of it was the wife's taste and all of it she got when we split. The house on Mountain Falls Road was something I'd wanted real bad when the wife and I were married, but she never liked it so we didn't buy it. I guess some guys might call that pussy-whipped, I always just called it survival. That woman had a mean mouth on her.

But after I got to know the house, when Laura lived there, I loved it even more. And now it was mine, but if things kept me in Houston much longer, there was the possibility I might just lose it. And the thought of losing it kinda took away the sting that had been in the house ever since I'd moved in, the stinging memory of Laura. Because now the house meant more to me than Laura did.

And I started thinking about ways of fixing it up, and saving up money for furniture of my very own, and maybe even buying a picture or two for the walls. I figured I didn't have to be a decorator to make my own house look good, right?

But that wasn't to be yet, not with Jewel still in the hospital and still under suspicion of murder. When I got back to Jewel's house that afternoon, after the doctor said he'd call the police and tell them what Jewel had said, Sergeant Lincoln was waiting for me in the driveway.

I figured under normal circumstances, this was a nice kid. Maybe even a good cop, though I've heard things about the Houston Police Department that would keep me from sending them my résumé in any kind of all-fired rush. But like any cop with an apparent open-and-shut case, he wasn't real happy about these complications the doctor and Honey and I were throwing at him.

When he saw me drive up, he got out of his unmarked car and stood there, waiting for me to get out of mine. When I did, he looked down at me with that two-inch superiority of his, held out his hand, and I shook it. He said, "Doesn't change anything, Milt."

"What's that, David?"

"My only alternative is to figure your sister is lying."

"Well, now I figure a lot of people coming out of a coma are able to come up with an instant lie, don't you?"

He shook his head. "I know she's your sister and you don't wanna think she done this, but..."

I shook my head. "No thinking about it, David. She said she didn't do it. She doesn't even know Henry's dead. She says there was someone with Henry when she got home from the store. Now I hate to burst your bubble and make you do any actual work, but chances are pretty damn good that somebody else did the deed."

"You gonna invite me into the house or we gonna stand out here playing Mexican stand-off and freezing our balls off?"

I grinned. "Only if you got an open mind."

He grinned back and shrugged. "I'll listen, Milt. But I'm not promising anything."

Once inside the house and settled in the den with beers in hand, I said, "You know anything about TPD Oil?"

"I know your brother-in-law worked for 'em."

"His secretary's disappeared."

"You wanna file a missing person's?"

I shrugged. "Not yet. I wanna know where she is, though. And I wanna know why she disappeared only minutes after talking with me in the cemetery."

Lincoln was a good cop. His ears perked up. "What'd she tell you?"

Now this was where it was gonna get sticky. Because, actually, all she told me was a great big reason why Jewel would want her husband dead. I skirted the issue, trying to bring up my theory about TPD and Henry's position as accountant.

"Yeah, but what did the secretary tell you?" Give a dog a bone and he's gonna chew it till the flavor's all gone, I swear to God.

"Nothing much," I said.

"What?"

So I figured the best thing to do under the circumstances was give him a little bee in his bonnet about possible jealous husbands and let him work on that a while while I worked on TPD. You do what you gotta do, know what I mean?

He shook his head. "Come on, Milt. A guy's insured for five hundred thousand dollars, screws around on his wife, and that's a reason for somebody else to have offed him? Give me a break."

So I told him all about the fact that Jewel didn't care for Henry all that much and probably wouldn't have minded.

"Not minded? I don't care if she hated the guy; there's such a thing as pride, Milt. A lady finds out her husband's screwing anything that walks, hurts her pride, right?"

"Fine. Okay. So she blows his brains out. But why try to kill herself?"

"Afraid of getting caught."

"My sister's not stupid, David. She could have figured out something else. She wouldn't have tried to kill herself over Henry's infidelity."

"Shame? Embarrassment? No end of reasons why she'd do it. Sorry, this just don't wash."

"You're bound and determined to lock up my sister, aren't you?" I shook my head and felt a little bit helpless. "You got no idea how wrong you are."

He stood up to go. "We're going to indict her. Thought you'd want to know. As soon as the doctor says she's able." He walked to the door and I followed. "Now, Milt, one other thing. I know you been messing around with this, trying to come up with somebody else who did it. Well, take it from me, nobody else did. So keep your nose clean. You're a long way from your jurisdiction. I don't want you running around the city accusing people and sticking your nose into TPD business. I don't know how they run things in Oklahoma, but here in Houston, we prefer it if the actual Houston police do the work, ya know? If I was you, I'd take the kids on back to Oklahoma and come back when it's time for the trial. Your sister's not going anywhere."

He didn't try to shake my hand this time, which I figured showed he wasn't as big a fool as he tried to act.

But I had one big question that I wanted one big answer to: Where the hell was Debbie Meeker and why the hell had she run off like that? Okay, so it's two questions, but I still wanted answers and I didn't know how to go about getting them. Then I remembered that Debbie had mentioned another lady, one of Henry's old flames who'd gotten herself engaged. What was her name? Barbara. Barbara Almon. I just hoped to hell she didn't leave TPD when she got married, then I figured women didn't do that much anymore. You have a good job, you don't leave it just 'cause you found Mr. Right. Not unless Mr. Right is independently wealthy. I just hoped to hell Barbara Almon's Mr. Right was a working stiff.

So I sat down in the den and pulled the phone to me to dial TPD and realized I didn't remember the phone number and, as I'm a lazy son of a bitch and Honey wasn't there to find the phone book for me, I dialed information, got the number, and called TPD.

This time, while I was on hold, the Muzak was playing "Okie from Miscogie" with a full string orchestra, I swear to God. But I didn't have to listen to much of it before I had me Barbara Almon on the phone.

I explained to her who I was and, although she was a little bit skeptical about it, she agreed to meet me for lunch the next day.

That evening I had a job to do. Breaking it to my baby sister that her husband had shuffled off this mortal coil. Or whatever. As a peace officer, this is a job I've done before. More often than I'd like.

You get all kinds of reactions, not a one of 'em good. You got your screamers, the ones that start screaming before you got your spiel half way out, you got your stiff-upper-lippers (they're the ones most likely to blow up later in a way not as therapeutic as screaming, like suicide or homicide), and you got what I like to classify as the "No shit"'s. The one's who look at you like, "No Shit? Bubba's dead, huh? How much insurance was he carrying, Officer?''

The worst was when I had to tell Bernie Spreen that his little girl Beth Anne had been killed with a carload of girls going way too fast down Highway 5 on Saturday night. They'd been playing tag with a carload of boys and the girl driving, Patti Alexander, had flipped her little Pinto end over end going around a curve. The boys had managed to pull out all but two of the girls before the gas tank blew. Travis Braumbutten's little girl Nina had been thrown clear enough that she just got burned over fifty percent of her body. But Beth Anne Spreen stayed inside.

Bernie was a stiff-upper-lipper. When I went to his door to tell him, he just pushed me aside and walked stiff-legged to his Oldsmobile in the driveway. I'd known Bernie Spreen my whole life and we'd always been friends so I just followed him out to the scene 'cause I knew that's where he was going. All the girls had been taken by ambulance to the hospital but some of the boys were still hanging around, trying to help, I guess. Bernie went up to one of 'em, him not even really knowing what had happened, and began beating on him. Took me and two firemen to pull him off the boy. The boy hadn't even been the driver. But I guess Bernie just needed to hit something handy.

No matter how you do it, telling somebody that someone they love is dead still makes you the bearer of bad tidings, and if half of 'em had a gun you'd be dead before you got out the "I'm sorry"'s. I'd even had to do it with a family member, Jewel herself, when I called her long-distance to tell her Mama was dead. But she'd been expecting that.

But that evening in Houston was something else again. Dr. Hussain and I went into Jewel's room and she was just lying there like always, tubes running in and out, but the emerald eyes shone at us and there was a little bitty old smile on her face. Until we told her that Henry was dead. She didn't say much, just sorta waved her hand, trying to brush the words away.

"The kids," she said. "How are the kids?"

"They're okay," I told her, "just worried about you."

"Who did it?" she asked.

"You remember the visitor you spoke of? Can you tell us about that?"

"What visitor?" she asked. And that's when the doctor broke it off. She was getting agitated and couldn't take any more questions. And now she didn't seem to remember what she'd said earlier. About the visitor. Wonderful.

So I left the hospital feeling about as low as a body could feel and still be above ground and went on home to Jewel's house to try to get some sleep.

The next day, at noon, I went to the restaurant near the downtown building that housed TPD Oil to meet Barbara Almon. I'm not what you'd call a conspiracy buff. I don't run around wondering who hired Lee Harvey Oswald and how he connected to Jack Ruby. I always figured John Wilkes Booth was just another crazy actor. But you gotta wonder about the "awl bidness." You really do. I mean, one day we were all standing in line for a gallon or two of gas every other Wednesday of a full moon, the next day there's so goddamn much oil half the Southwest's out of a job.

I knew this fella, personally, who worked at a refinery. He said they had three of those great big old tanks and in all the twenty-two years he worked there, they'd only had one full and one partial. The third always had just a little in the bottom to keep it healthy. But he says during the oil shortage, and this is the God's honest truth, all three of them tanks were filled to the brim. About eleven or twelve million gallons of ready-to-sell unleaded.

And then, all of a sudden, when the price has got up to over a dollar a gallon, glory be, there's gas a plenty. So damn much gas and oil that, well, fellas, we're just not making the profit we used to, so we're gonna have to lay off some working stiffs. And maybe get rid of some of these little fellas, the ones that think they can own their own company. Can't have none of that, now can we. So the big guys start to squeeze and the little guy's back where he oughta been all along, the unemployment line.

Now that's the way I figure it. Course, I'm prejudiced. I come from oil country where a lot of people I know who were almost making it ain't making it at all now. And I figure, with TPD being a shy smaller than Exxon and Texaco, what the hell are they doing still in business? How come they didn't go bust with everybody else? And I figure, that's kinda funny, them not going bust, and it's also kinda funny, in a peculiar sort of way, not a ha-ha sort of way, that their main accountant, namely my brother-in-law, got himself shot by person or persons unknown. I don't think I'm being a conspiracy buff here, I think I'm just looking at the facts.

Well, I got to the restaurant and, I swear to God, with a woman like my sister at home, I did have to wonder about Henry's taste in the ladies. Barbara

Almon was a big ole gal and not much of the big was muscle. But she had a way about her, I'll say that. In her early twenties, probably, she had more energy than she oughta for carrying that much weight. She bounced and giggled and grinned, pouted and wiggled and tapped her foot and I gotta admit for just half a second there I had to wonder what it would be like in bed with a great big dynamo like Barbara Almon. But I was there on the business of freeing my baby sister so I didn't think long about such things.

"I had a little talk with Debbie Meeker before she took off," I told her. "She tells me you used to be involved with Henry for a while."

She shook her mane of carrot red hair that had to add another ten pounds to her bulk. "She shouldn't oughta told you that," she said pouting. "That's none of anybody's business 'cept me and Henry."

"Your boyfriend know about you and Henry?"

She grinned and bounced a few times in her seat and I stole a look at the management to see if they were worried about their chair. They didn't appear to be. "Henry introduced me to Ogden. Oggie knew all about me and Henry. He didn't mind a bit."

"You know where Debbie Meeker ran off to?"

She squirmed and frowned and tossed her hair. "Golly, I wish I did. She promised to give me a bridal shower! Now I don't know what I'm supposed to do. Wait to hear from her or just get somebody else to do it? What do you think, Mr. Kovak?"

I shrugged. "You know where Debbie was from, Barbara? Where her parents live?"

Again she frowned and placed one pudgy finger against one of her ample chins. Then came the hair toss, the giggle, and the shrug. "Golly, I'm not sure. Some little bitty ole place, though, I think." Dropping her voice to a stage whisper, she said, "Debbie was a bit of a hick."

As a bit of a hick myself, I tried not to take offense. "Think, Barbara. She ever mention it?"

She gave me her studied thinking look for half a second, then said, "Port Charles. I'm sure of it. You know where that is?"

I denied the knowledge and she explained. "It's down near the coast, one of those stinky refinery towns."

"Know what her daddy's name is?" I asked.

She shrugged. "Golly, no. Why would I?"

Why, indeed. I thanked her and watched her walk off, all two hundred young, vital, alive pounds of her and figured Oggie was probably a lucky man, if it didn't kill him.

It was only a little after one o'clock in the afternoon when I left Barbara Almon and, as After Hours was on my way home, sorta, I decided to stop by. This early in the afternoon, the place was almost empty, with only one patron at the bar, a man who could have been anywhere between fifty and one hundred, with the red, bulbous nose of a heavy drinker, and the frayed shirt collar and run down shoes of an out-of-work heavy drinker. He didn't even glance up when I opened the door and walked in.

"Afternoon," the bartender called.

"Afternoon," I answered, "Al, right?"

"That's right. I know you?"

"I was in here the other night asking questions about Henry Hotchkiss."

"Oh, yeah, right. The cop with the cute little partner."

I cleared my throat. "Yeah. That's right."

"You here to ask more about Henry's women?"

"Naw. I'm here for a beer. A light beer if you got one."

"One? Fuck. Got about a hundred different brands." He began reading off his list of light beers and I stopped him at a Miller. The only one I'd heard of. "You want a glass?"

"Bottle's fine." I settled down at the bar with the longneck and took a deep swig. "Beer's best when it's hot outside," I said, "but there's something reassuring about it when it's cold out there, too."

"Never trusted a man who didn't drink beer."

"Ain't that the truth."

"Figure any man who won't share a beer with you's gotta be a communist."

"Let me buy you a beer, Al."

"Thank you. Don't mind if I do." He opened a Bud and took a swig. "You like that light stuff?"

"Ya get used to it. First time I drank it, thought it tasted like piss and water, but now..."

"Tastes like water and piss?" Al said, and cracked his ownself up.

I laughed. "It's okay. Helped me lose a little weight."

Al looked down at his own gut protruding over the white apron he wore over his chino pants. "That a fact?"

"Yeah. Got me a divorce and figured maybe I'd better start thinking about things like my weight."

"Yeah. I got me a divorce too couple years back. First thing I did was go out and buy a rug for this," he said, pointing to his shiny dome.

"Interesting kinda rug you got there."

He laughed fit to beat the devil. "Shit. I hated that thing! Took me forever to get it on, then took off half my skin getting the damned thing off. Never fooled nobody either. Then one day this woman comes up to me and hands me an article right here in this bar. Article says how scientific survey's proved baldheaded men are better lovers. I took that damned thing off right here and threw it in the trash. Ever since then, all's I do is spray a little Pledge on my head once every morning, buff if up real good, and smile at the ladies!"

I grinned and drained my beer. "Pledge, huh?"

"Lemon-scented."

"Might be using that myself pretty soon." I put some bills down on the counter and started for the door, only to hear a door in the back open up and see the sweet young thing from my last visit, the barhop, come strolling in from the back.

"Hey, Lisa, 'bout time," Al called.

"I'm a minute early, old man, and don't you forget it. I want my overtime!" She saw me and smiled. "Well, hey, there."

I grinned and walked over to her. "Hey, yourself."

"How you doing?" she asked.

"Fine. How are you?"

Now, I read this book once about body language and I might not remember a lot of it, but seems to me I do remember that what she was doing, that being namely having one hand on her hip and one hand resting lightly on my chest, was an indication of flirtation. At least I hoped like hell that was so.

"Oh, I'm fine," she answered. "Milt, right?"

"Yeah. That's right."

"I was hoping you'd come around here again."

"Well, here I am."

"Yeah. So you are."

"Lisa! You working or what?" Al the bartender called out.

"Shit," Lisa said under her breath to me. "Yeah, yeah! I'm coming." She turned back to me. "You gonna be around later?"

I shrugged. "I don't know. Maybe."

She smiled and wiggled her fingers on my shirt-front. "Hope so." And she was off, walking that walk back toward the bar. I tried taking the foolish grin off my face, failed, and just left.

Later that afternoon, with the kids in their rooms doing their homework, or at least pretending to, with two jamboxes going full blast behind closed doors, I asked Honey if she knew where Port Charles was.

She told me, then said, "Why?"

"Because that's where Debbie Meeker was from. I wanna go down there and see if I can find her."

She shook her head and looked at me like a mama might look at a slightly stupid child. "Milt, you following up on this wild goose chase? This TPD conspiracy?"

"It's all I got."

"Hell, Milt. We know it had to be about Henry's phildandering."

"No, we don't. I went down every avenue there was on that, Honey, and I didn't find diddly. Now I'm trying something new."

"Okay." She shrugged. "So when do we go?"

"What's this we shit? I don't recollect having a turd in my pocket."

"Very funny. I'm going with you and you already know that."

Which I did. "Tomorrow? Can we get there and back before the kids get home from school?"

"Depends on how long it takes us once we're there. They'll be okay until Chuck gets home from work. But I got some things to do tomorrow. How about the day after?"

I agreed and we made our plans, but I had to admit to myself that driving that far alone with Honey Lancaster was going to be a trial.

That night, though, a funny thing happened. Right after dinner, I got a phone call.

"Milt?"

"Yes?" It was a sweet voice, one I recognized but I wasn't sure where from.

"This is Lisa. From After Hours?"

"Well, hey, Lisa. What can I do for you?"

"Tomorrow's my night off and I was wondering if maybe you could meet me for a drink? Any place but After Hours."

Part of me was thinking maybe she had more information about Henry on her mind, and part of me was replaying what I'd learned in the body language book, so I agreed and made plans to meet her the next evening around eight o'clock.

"Well, good, then. I'm looking forward to it," she said.

"Me, too," I said.

I heard a shout from the bar area through the phone and Lisa say, "All right! Jesus, give me a break!" To me, she said, "Milt, honey, I gotta go. See you tomorrow." And we rang off.

A couple of hours later, I got the kids ready for bed and was headed for the bathroom myself when the doorbell rang, not just once but several times in succession. "Well, Christ on a bicycle!" I muttered and headed for the door, hearing the footsteps of six smaller feet behind me. I opened the door to a very excited Asian lady.

"Baby! Come! Baby hurt! Come!" She grabbed my arm and started pulling on me.

"What's the matter, ma'am?" I asked, resisting her tug on my sleeve. "What baby? What's happening?"

"Car! My baby! Come! Now! Come!" She kept tugging at my arm. It was black as pitch outside so I told Leonard over my shoulder to get me a flashlight. The pressure on my arm lessened and I looked back to see the Asian lady running out of the circle of light thrown by the front porch lamp.

"Lady! Wait! I'm coming!" I yelled into the darkness and turned to find Leonard handing me the flashlight.

"Need some help?" he asked.

"Just stay here. If it's real bad, I'll holler at you to call 911, Okay?"

"Yes, sir."

I turned on the flashlight and followed its beam to the end of the driveway, circling around a van parked in front of Honey and Chuck's house. As I got even with the side door of the van, all hell broke loose.

EIGHT

WHAT FELT LIKE about forty NFL linebackers jumped astraddle me and started trying to beat what little brains I got to a pulp. I got in a few licks with the heavy-duty flashlight, hard enough to break the bulb anyway, so that what little I could see was now completely gone. I felt my kidneys trying to rearrange themselves, felt a rib crack, tried to scream, only to have it cut off midway by a heavy blow to the belly, knocking the wind right out of me. I doubled over, just in time to be straightened up by a fist in my face.

I fell up against the van and slid down it, spitting blood out as I went down. My eyes were beginning to adjust to the darkness and I just barely saw a kick aimed at my head and fell to my right, avoiding it everywhere but my spine. Still and all, the pain shot threw most of my body. I tried yelling again, but all I got was a gagging, sputtering sound from all the blood in my mouth. My ears were ringing and I thought, "I'm gonna die on a residential street in goddamn Houston, Texas." It was a sad thought, indeed.

Then I started hearing things other than the beating of my own blood. A high whining sound, the crunch of metal on metal, a screech, a yell, a yip of pain, then saw four pairs of feet running by me and heard a voice sounding a lot like Chuck's saying, "What the fuck's going on out here?" Then the little support I was getting from the van vanished as the motor started and the van roared off, flinging me further onto my right side.

I looked up to see my baby sister's children gathered around me, Leonard with a fireplace tool in his hand, the end of it shiny from something wet that I hoped was one of my assailant's blood, Carl standing there with his little league baseball bat, and Marlene with a spray bottle of ammonia.

"Shit! We got 'em. You see that, Uncle Chuck?"

"Jesus! Milt! Man, you okay?" Chuck hauled me to my feet none too gently and looked at me. "Man, you're a fucking mess."

"Tank you veddy mush," I said around the blood.

"I got 'em right in the eyes with this!" Marlene said. "Won't surprise me a bit if they find that van wrecked!"

"I got one of 'em in the knee!" Carl said proudly.

"Yeah, and one of 'em's bleeding like a stuck pig," Leonard proclaimed.

"Who?" Chuck demanded. "What the fuck happened?"

The kids all started in at once, telling the tale, while I stood there bleeding. Then I saw a beam of light jiggling down the front walk of Honey and Chuck's house.

"Chuck? What in blazes is going on? My God, Milton, what have they done to you?" Honey said, all in one breath.

"I gone spiph," I managed, and spat out a heap of blood all over my own feet. Everybody backed off a little which I thought was a might unfeeling.

"Chuck, damnit!" Honey said. "Get this man in the house now!"

So Chuck started to pick me up but I managed to convey to him that I could walk okay and if he tried picking me up again his manhood would be in a heap of trouble. With Chuck's and Leonard's arms as aids, I managed to get into Honey and Chuck's house.

Sitting on the commode in their hall bath, with old sheets covering the bathmats and floor so as not to be dirtied by my bodily fluids, Honey set about minding my wounds.

"My teef," I said.

"I beg your pardon?" she said, staring in my mouth.

"My teef. Loz my teef?"

"No. You still got all your 'teef', but what you also got is a big ole hole in the inside of your cheek." She stood back and stared at me for a minute, then mused aloud, "How in the hell do you put a Band-Aid on the inside of someone's mouth?"

"Cotter..." I spit into the sink and Honey winced. "Cotton balls. Like a dentist."

"Sounds good to me." She left the room and came back in a minute with a package of cotton balls. "These are for makeup so they're not sterile. Think that'll be okay?"

I shrugged, visions of staph infections floating through my mind. She stuffed a couple of the cotton balls up against the inside of my cheek and said, "How's that?"

"Uga—"

Giggling, she said, "You look just like Marlon Brando in *The Godfather*!"

"Ank oo." I pantomimed writing.

"Word games, Milton?" But she nonetheless graciously left the room and returned with a pad of paper and a ballpoint. I scribbled "police."

"Chuck's on the phone right now with your Sergeant Lincoln."

I wrote, "He coming over?"

"I don't know," Honey answered, "but I'll go find out. Any other wounds?"

I scribbled, "Ribs."

"We'd better get you to the hospital, Milt. I mean it."

I wrote, "Ace bandage."

"I don't know how to do it! I'm not a goddamn nurse, Milton!"

I wrote, "Did in high school. All the time. Bad ball player. Lots of injuries."

"Well, speaking of bad ball players, Chuck should know how to do that. Soon as he's off the phone, I'll get him to come wrap you up. If you're sure you don't want to go to the hospital."

I nodded emphatically and she left in search of her ex-jock. In the time it took me to wonder who in the hell had beaten me up and why the hell they'd done it, Chuck and Honey were both in the bathroom with me. It wasn't that big a bathroom and I worried about the air supply. Chuck opened the medicine cabinet and began rummaging around in it.

"I know I got me some Ace bandages in here someplace. Here they are. Okay, Milt. Strip off that shirt."

I looked guardedly at Honey. "It's okay, Milt. You seen one hairy chest you seen 'em all," she said.

I was very conscious at first of the roll around my middle the light beer hadn't completely eroded, but the pain of lifting the shirt over my head shot vanity right out of my mind. We spent some time, me with my arms up in the air, Honey and Chuck trying to wrap the damn bandage around me and trying not to get in each other's way.

"Chuck move!"

"Fuck, woman, I can't get this with your cute little ass sticking out here!"

"Just leave my ass out of this and hand me the other end there..."

"Well, take it..."

"I've got it, I've got it!"

Finally, we managed to get me wrapped up and my shirt back on. I shooed them out and spit the cotton out. The bleeding appeared to have stopped. I joined the others in Honey and Chuck's living room just as the doorbell chimed. Chuck went to the door.

"Don't go off with any Asian women," I said.

"Huh?" he replied.

But the person at the door wasn't a frantic Asian woman, it was a sleepy Sergeant Lincoln.

"You look like shit, Milt," he said as he walked in the door.

"Fuck you," I said.

Every mouth in the room opened and every eye was on me. "Excuse me, I've had a rough night."

"What happened?" David Lincoln asked.

So I set about telling him, then the kids joined in when their turn came, and to my chagrin I found out my forty NFL linebackers were in reality only two pint-sized Asian men.

"Probably used karate," I mumbled but nobody seemed to notice.

"So, they steal anything?"

"No."

"So, what'd they want?"

"Damned if I know."

"So, you wanna file a report?"

"I wanna take a bath, actually."

Lincoln stood up and headed for the door. "Well, I guess I'm glad you're alive."

"Thank you."

"No. I mean . . . shit, I don't know what I mean. Look man"—he patted me on the arm—"sorry this had to happen in my town, but you know how it goes.''

"Right. Thanks for coming over." We all stood up and headed for the door when I said, ''But you know, David, there had to be a reason for this. I mean, I haven't exactly taken your advice about not asking around about TPD. For example, just today I talked to one of their employees. And this evening somebody beats the snot out of me.''

''Milt, I had a rough day. I'm tired. I was asleep when your friend here called me. All I want to do is crawl back in bed with my wife and hope she don't wake up. I don't wanna hear your conspiracy theories. Not now. Not tonight. Do me that one little favor, okay?'' He walked out the door. Turning back he said, ''Not every crime in this city is connected to you, Kovak. Know what I mean?''

With those words of wisdom, he left. When I looked around at my friends and family, my support system, if you will, not one of 'em would look me in the eye. But, shit, it was a theory, right?

I got the kids and headed out the door, saying my thank yous to Honey and Chuck. As David Lincoln started his car, I opened the door to our house and ushered the kids in. Then spent about an hour soaking in Epsom salts in a hot bath.

I recuperated the next day, lazing around the house doing my imitation of my cat Evinrude after one of his rape-and-pillage expeditions. Around noon, I got a call from somebody telling me I'd just won "one of the following prizes." I hung up the phone. I knew in my heart the prize I'd won was probably a three day all-expenses-paid vacation to Bora Bora. All I had to come up with was the plane fare. Or a food processor that I could have free of charge after sitting through only a two-hour sales pitch to buy condo timeshares. The food processor, of course, would turn out to be two paring knives.

There are certain words and phrases, "You've just won one of the following prizes" being high up there on the list, that I've learned to avoid at all costs in my almost fifty years. Words like chocolatey, buttery, meaty, or any other "ee" word. Or restaurants that call themselves "Mom's," or advertise their food as "just like Grandma used to make," or call it "home cooking." And anything, other than beer, of course, that uses the word "lite."

I make it a habit to stay away from anything that's "new and improved," "easy-open," "all natural," or "organic." I'd never look at a house advertised as "homey," "roomy," "cost-efficient," "charming," or "space-saving." And I always avoid people who say things like "down home," "for your own good," "take it under advisement," or, the worst one of all, "trust me." Somehow, all those words and phrases are as reassuring as going out on a blind date with a lady with a "wonderful personality."

But my date that evening wasn't blind and her personality wasn't what I was interested in. I fed the kids and sent them over to Chuck and Honey's and ended up downtown at a little fern bar whose name I didn't notice.

Now, I'm generally a modest man, but I got to tell you, I was right about the body language and Henry wasn't what little Lisa had on her mind. The fern bar I met her at was on the ground floor of an old apartment house where Lisa lived. And after one quick beer, and quicker sympathy over my injuries, she invited me upstairs for a second.

There were four doors on that second floor, leading I presumed to four apartments. Lisa's apartment was really only two rooms. The first was the living room, kitchen, and dining room, the placing of furniture separating the areas. The second was the bedroom and bathroom. The bathroom had no door or walls. It was just the necessary appliances along one wall of the bedroom. Except for the bathtub. The bathtub was in the kitchen area. Urban chic, I guess.

"Sit down and make yourself at home," she said, indicating some low, foam rubber furniture. I sank my nearly fifty-year-old body down and hoped there wasn't a fire anytime soon because I wasn't sure I could get up again. The walls were decorated with posters of rock stars, not one of whom I recognized. The only way I knew they were rock stars, or thought they might be, was the guitars they were holding. Remember, I'm a trained detective.

She removed two beers from the old-fashioned icebox and brought them into the living area and sank down next to me. Handing me a beer, her hand touched mine for longer than was absolutely necessary.

"So," I said, clearing my throat, "you have some more information on Henry?"

She cocked her head at an angle and grinned. "No. That the only reason you came up here, Milt?"

"Well, no." I grinned back. "I gotta admit I like the company."

"You wanna fuck?"

"Okay."

That's how I found out about the bathroom fixtures being along the bedroom wall. I gotta admit I just barely noticed that. She picked up something off a stack of things on the sink and handed it to me. I looked at it. It was a cherry-flavored condom. Now don't that beat all?

Up until that night, I'd only been with three women in my life (not counting this lady of questionable repute I met in a bar outside of White Plains that thought it was real funny being with an almost-twenty-year-old male virgin Airman Third Class, but that's not something I talk about much)—my wife, Laura, and Glenda Sue. And all three of them had been my idea. Lisa was a different matter entirely. I'd never been seduced before, if you don't mind stretching a point a bit and calling what she did seduction, and I gotta say I liked it. Give me an aggressive woman any old day of the week. We men have been seducing women in one fashion or another for a long time now, but having the tables turned on me was a very pleasant, if painful, surprise. Take it from me, making love with a broken rib's not what it's cracked up to be. Sorry about the pun.

We lay there on her bed and I had to ask, being a detective after all, "How come you and Henry never ... you know ... ?"

"What? How come I never fucked Henry? 'Cause if I fucked you, then shit, it just follows I'd fuck anybody, right?"

"Well, no, that's not what I meant..."

"You need to do something about your self-esteem, Milt."

"No, what I meant..."

"Actually, you heard of love at first sight, right?"

I was worried about this girl's train of thought, but I answered, "Yes..."

"Well, with Henry and me it was hate at first sight. With both of us. Just pure, instant dislike...no, stronger. Hate. I figure he was my executioner in my past life."

"Huh?"

She sat up in bed, her naked breasts dancing above me. "I was hanged in a past life. Didn't I tell you?"

"Ah, no..."

"Of course I was innocent!"

"Ah, yeah..."

"I figure Henry was either the prosecutor or the executioner. Don't you think?"

"Ah, maybe..."

"Besides," she said, lying down next to me, "he was shorter than me."

Oh, well, I thought, go figure.

We stopped talking for a while and I left her place around midnight and headed home. After all was said and done, I tried my damnedest to feel cheap and used, but it just didn't work. It took me the rest of the night to wipe the smile off my face. And it wasn't till driving home that I even thought about things like herpes, AIDS, nasty stuff like that. But then I thought that that was probably why she had that stack of condoms. Then I grinned to myself and thought, "Milton, you old fox, you just practiced safe sex." I heard that term on Oprah one day. Now here I was doing it.

And the next day, driving to Port Charles with Honey wasn't as bad as I'd thought it would be. I just kept thinking about the night before and trying not to giggle.

NINE

AFTER SEEING Port Charles, Texas, I apologized mentally to Houston for everything I'd thought about it. It's a mean little town, Port Charles. I figured when the oil business was ripe and Port Charles was booming, it was probably even worse. Row after row of refineries and a smell that would gag a maggot, I swear to God.

But there didn't seem to be much left of the town now, some refineries shut down, most of the others on partial workforces and most of the people who remained were out of work. Stores closed in the downtown area, men sitting on the windowsills of the boarded-up shops, smoking cigarettes and wondering what to do with themselves. A flat town, not a hill anywhere that wasn't man-made and didn't have to do with a freeway.

It was overcast that day as Honey and I drove around, looking for the address we'd found in the phone book for Norton Meeker. There had been a Norton, a J. R., and a Truman Meeker and having called J. R. first, being in an alphabetical frame of mind, I'd found out that Norton Meeker was Debbie's daddy. J.R. was Debbie's daddy's first cousin, and Truman was Debbie's daddy's brother. That I understood, being a small town fella myself.

We pulled up in front of the Meeker home and I looked around. Just like Jewel's neighborhood, this one had a lot of dead houses. The Meeker home itself was a small frame affair, not unlike most of the houses in my town of Longbranch, just a little seedier looking, or maybe that's my own prejudice. The yellow paint that had been brushed on years before was peeling bad, shutters were loose, and the lawn consisted mostly of winter-dead Johnson grass. We left the car on the street and walked up the driveway, crunching on the oyster shells laid down instead of gravel, up to the front door, and knocked.

A lady of about fifty answered the door, hair done up in a Pentecostal-type hairdo with lots of ringlets and such. She was dressed in a midcalf skirt and high-collared blouse and her shoes were about as sensible as you could get this side of a pair of Red Wings.

"Morning, ma'am," I said. "My name's Milton Kovak" —I flashed my badge quickly—"and I'm looking for your daughter, Debbie."

Mrs. Meeker frowned. "Is Debbie Anne in some sort of trouble, Officer?"

I smiled. "No, ma'am, I just need to ask her some questions. As I'm sure she told you, her boss was killed..."

"Oh, my!" Mrs. Meeker looked like she was about to faint and I realized Debbie had neglected to mention Henry's death to her mama.

Honey took Mrs. Meeker by the arm and led her into the living room of the house and sat her down on the sofa. And I gotta tell you, that was the plainest room I'd ever been in. There was the sofa, a straight-backed chair, and a picture of Jesus. And that was it. The room was lit by a glaring overhead light fixture and the walls were painted a dead white. The windows were covered in plain white pull-down shades with no frills. And they were pulled down tight in the middle of the day. There wasn't a book, magazine, or newspaper to be seen. No TV, no radio, no nothing.

Honey rubbed Mrs. Meeker's hands and said, "You okay now, ma'am?"

The lady gathered herself up and said, "Mr. Jamison was killed?"

Honey and I looked at each other. "Mr. Jamison?" I asked.

"Debbie Anne's boss."

I heard the back door open and bang close and a well-remembered voice said, "Mama? Where's lunch? I'm starved!"

Sticking her head into the living room, Debbie saw Honey and I and turned a bright red.

"Hey, Mr. Kovak," she said, and the only word to describe it has to be sheepishly, whatever the hell that means.

"Hey, Debbie. I've been looking for you."

"Mama, you wanna go fix lunch while I talk to these people?"

"Debbie Anne," her mother said slightly breathless, "they say Mr. Jamison's been killed."

And Debbie said "What?" and Honey and I both said "No..." all at the same time.

Then Debbie shooed her mama out of the room, telling her she only had so long for lunch, if she didn't mind, and that Mr. Jamison was just fine and dandy. Her mama left, a little hesitant, saying, "But, but..." over her shoulder a lot.

After her mother had left the room and Debbie had closed the door that shut off the living room from the rest of the house, she and Honey sat on the sofa while I managed to finagle my butt into the straight-backed chair.

Leaning toward me, her voice a whisper, Debbie said, "What in the hell are you doing here?"

"Who's Mr. Jamison?" I asked instead of answering. Answering a question with a question is one of those tricks you learn in Cops 101.

"My boss! My new boss! Jeez, you almost gave Mama a stroke! Mr. Jamison's real big in the church and you made Mama think he was dead!"

"She doesn't know about Henry?" I asked.

Debbie sighed and leaned back against the sofa. "Mama wouldn't understand about that. She thought it was plenty wicked me just moving to Houston. If she'd found out my boss had been killed by his wife for messing around, she'd have me in church eight hours a day instead of just two."

Before Honey could protest that her boss hadn't been killed by his wife, I said, "Why'd you leave in such a Godawful hurry?"

Debbie shrugged. "I got to thinking after I talked to you in the cemetery that I just couldn't face going back to that secretarial pool. I really hated it. Mama had been harping on me to come home and go to work for Mr. Jamison, so I figured there was no time like the present."

I avoided Honey's glance, which had to have a lot of "I told you so" in it.

But I'm a lot like a dog with a bone myself, and this was one bone I didn't want to let go of in an all-fired rush. "Debbie, what can you tell me about TPD?" I asked. I heard Honey sigh but ignored it.

"Like what?" Debbie asked.

"Like how come they made it through the oil crunch while other companies the same size bit the big one?"

She shrugged. "Oh, TPD's real diversified. They'd gotten into the distribution of personal computers big enough before the crunch to let that carry them through. We're...I mean they're...the sole U.S. distributor for Kami-Sen Systems. They're Japanese, ya know? The oil side is almost nonexistent now. And Mr. Durang, he's the guy that really owns TPD mostly, he's got his hand in lots of different things. Mostly thanks to Henry. He's gonna miss Henry a hell of a lot. Henry really knew his investments."

"So," I asked, "you see this Mr. Durang before you took off?"

Debbie frowned. "No. Why?"

"Just wondering how much severance pay he gave you."

"Like I told you, Mr. Kovak, I just left. I got some pay coming to me but I gotta call personnel and tell 'em. Why would Mr. Durang pay me? All that's supposed to come from personnel."

"Yeah," I said, doing my best sly smile, "I suppose it's *supposed to*."

"Well, now, what's that supposed to mean?"

"Milton..." Another county heard from.

"I'm just wondering why, on the day you and I talked, why you'd just up and leave all of a sudden like. I'm thinking maybe you had yourself a little talk with Mr. Durang..."

Debbie stood up. "You wanna get out of here now, Mr. Kovak?" she said. Her voice shaking. But so were my hands so I suppose we were even.

"Just trying to find out what the hell's going on, Debbie. Nothing personal."

"Nothing personal? My God, I think you just accused me of being in some conspiracy to kill Henry! Isn't that what you just did?"

"Well, now, no, not exactly..."

Honey stood up. "Milton, I think you've worn out your welcome here..."

"He sure as hell has!"

"Now, Debbie..."

She walked to the door and opened it.

"Sorry if I got you in any trouble with your mama, Debbie."

"Mr. Kovak, I know you're worried about your sister, and I don't blame you, but that gives you no call to come here accusing me—"

Her voice broke and she ran from the room. Honey pushed me out the door. Once in the car, she slammed her door real hard and ground the gears a little, and, I swear to God, if the verge of the road had been anything but oyster shell, she'd have left skid marks on her way out.

"You mad at me?" I asked.

"I can't believe you did that!"

"What?"

"What!? My, God, man, what the hell do you think you were doing back there? Jesus, what's wrong with you?"

"Well, you're the one insisting it's got to be . . . I believe the word you used was one of Henry's 'bimbos'?"

"You got no couth, Kovak, you know that?"

"I got a lotta couth. I got more couth in my little finger than you got . . ."

"Shut up, Kovak."

"Yes, ma'am."

Then, of all things, Honey started laughing. "Guess this shoots your conspiracy theory all to hell and gone!"

"Well, I'm just real glad you think this is so goddamn funny," I said. "Because now we're back to square one. If a jealous husband didn't do it and it hasn't got anything to do with Henry's job, then that leaves Jewel.''

Honey said, "You're as full of it as a Christmas turkey, you know that, Kovak?''

"You ever hear of the Yakusa?" I asked.

"What? That new Korean car?''

"No. It's a Japanese gang. Kinda like the Mafia.''

"So?''

"So I got beat up the other night by two Asian guys, right?''

"So?''

"So TPD's into computers now, right? *Japanese* computers?''

"Oh, for God's sake!''

"What?''

She just shut her mouth and drove. We were silent for a while, then I said, "We're on the same side, ya know?''

"Do you like shrimp?''

I didn't know what that had to do with the price of beans, but I said, "Yeah, I like shrimp.''

"Well, the only good thing about Port Charles's economy right now is you can get shrimp fairly cheap.''

I sat back and watched as she drove to an area on the Gulf where there were so many shrimp boats I felt like bursting into song. Except I couldn't remember the words. There was a little shack on a pier and a lot of Asian types running from shrimp boats moored at the dock to the shack carrying drums of something. The smell wasn't something you'd wanna write home to Mama about, but it beat the hell out of the cabbage and fart smells of the refineries.

"You stay here and I'll run in and dicker," she said.

I got out of the car and leaned against it while I waited, seeing what I could see. My state, Oklahoma hasn't got a hell of a lot of coastline, being a landlocked state, so I was impressed in spite of myself, although this wasn't exactly coastline. There was no surf, just brackish-looking shallow water.

A ways off I could see two men standing near a weird-looking boat, with one man inside the boat. The two guys were standing there, fully dressed, waist deep in the brackish-looking water, wearing heavy gloves and doing something weird. They'd reach down in the water and pull up lumps of dark gray-looking rock. They'd hand these lumps to the guy in the boat and he'd put 'em in a gunny sack on board. I finally figured out that these were some kind of ecology nuts cleaning up the water.

Honey came back with her purchases and walked over to where I stood by the pier railing.

"What're you looking at?" she asked.

"Those guys. I think they're biologists or something cleaning up the water."

Honey looked for a minute and then began laughing. "They're oystering, you fool."

"I knew that." I didn't look at her. "What's oystering?"

"See that lump of stuff? That's a whole bunch of oysters stuck together. They'll break 'em apart when they get it home. Law says something like six tow sacks is all you can take a day for private fishermen."

While we watched, one of the men standing in the water came up with a single oyster. Using a knife, he popped it open, and took a bottle out of his pocket. He sprinkled some of the contents of the bottle on the oyster and, using the knife to loosen it from the shell, slid the damn thing in his mouth. He threw the shell farther out in the water.

"Did that man just do what I think he did?" I asked Honey.

"Yeah. Bet that was Louisiana Red Hot in the bottle. My Daddy used to do that. Loved 'em fresh out of the water."

"You ready to leave?"

"Sure you don't wanna go back in the shack and see if they have some oysters?"

I walked with a lot of silence and a bunch of dignity to the car.

We got home about half an hour before school let out and I invited Honey in for a cup of coffee. She accepted. We took off our coats in the den and laid them on a chair and Honey sat down on the sofa while I went into the kitchen to put the kettle on. I turned on the gas and that's the last thing I remember.

I WOKE UP in the same hospital as Jewel, right down the hall. Of course, I didn't know that when I woke up. When I woke up, I wasn't sure what my name was or whether I was male or female. But seeing Honey sitting beside me with that worried look on her face let me know I was male in a big hurry.

"What happened?" I thought I asked.

Honey came to the bed with a damp rag and wet my lips. "What happened?" I repeated and this time she heard me.

"The stove blew up," she said. "You turned on a burner and the whole thing blew up."

"I don't remember smelling any gas," I croaked.

She shrugged. "Me neither. But that's in the hands of the arson squad now. Anyway, if you'll let me finish my heroic story. I dragged you out of the kitchen and got most of the fire out with Jewel's kitchen fire extinguisher before I called the ambulance. The kitchen's a mess and some windows are broken but other than that, no real damage."

"What about me?" I croaked.

"Well, you have a possible slight concussion and you probably won't need to shave for a while." She giggled. "You look funny."

I tried to get up with the express purpose of getting to a mirror to see how funny I looked and if I could remember what I looked like before. Honey pushed me back and dug in her purse and produced her compact mirror, which she held up for me to inspect my face.

Although my memory seemed to be a bit sketchy, I did remember distinctly having had eyebrows and eyelashes in the past. There were none now. My face was a strange shade of red, my eyes bloodshot, and my hairline had receded further than ever. I hoped it would be able to grow back.

Giving Honey back the mirror, I asked, "How'd I get the concussion?"

She shook her head. "It all happened so fast, Milt. I think the blast threw you up against the cabinets and that must have done it. How are you feeling?"

Since my head felt like if I shook it or nodded it I'd lose it, I held up my hand and wiggled it in a so-so gesture. That's when I noticed there was no hair on my hands or arms either. And they too were that ugly red color.

"Am I in pain?" I asked her.

She laughed. "Don't you know?"

I looked at my arms again. "They look like I should be, but I can't feel anything."

"Good. They've covered you with some sort of antiseptic goop that's supposed to take away the surface pain. I guess it's working."

"Is the antiseptic goop red?" I asked.

"No. Clear."

"Oh." I was red. Wonderful.

The door opened and Honey and I both turned to see who it was. David Lincoln marched in and looked at me.

"He alive?" he asked Honey.

She didn't answer and looked away.

"What are you doing here?" I asked Lincoln.

"Thought you'd want to know the arson squad just finished at your sister's place. They got their bomb squad boys to looking at it and they almost missed it. Took 'em about six hours to reconstruct the stove but they finally figured it out. The loot in charge said it was the slickest rig he'd ever seen.

Somebody drilled a tiny hole in the gas line leading to the stove burners and hooked up a thin-walled plastic tube to it with putty. The other end of the tube got fed down into the oven. Then—and this is the slick part—he taped the mouth of the tube into one of those big Hefty leaf bags tucked inside the oven and filled it up with gas. That's why you didn't smell any gas."

"But how did it explode when I turned it on?"

"Simple. That stove is one of those new ones with an electric spark gadget instead of an old-style pilot light. Our boy only had to hook up a couple of small wires to the On switch and tape them close together on the Hefty bag. When you turned on the burner, a spark jumped from one wire to the other, melted a hole in the bag, and blooey. The explosion would blow the wires away and the fire would melt the tube and Hefty bag to nothing. They would never have found it unless they were looking for it. Which they were. Sort of."

Not being able to help myself, I said, "You check and make sure my sister didn't remove her tubes, crawl out of the bed, and do it herself?"

Looking at Honey, Lincoln said, "I'm sure happy to see he hasn't lost his sparkling wit."

Honey crossed her arms over her nice little chest and didn't say anything, and wouldn't look at Sergeant Lincoln or even acknowledge his presence. I determined there and then to try my best not to ever get the lady mad at me. Hardly worth it.

"If this stove bomb was so slick," I said, "how come I'm still kicking?"

"Well," Lincoln said, tugging at his ear, "according to the bomb guys, *this person* was a little too impressed with the explosive force of a bag of gas. There just wasn't enough of a bang to do the job right. Sorry, I mean luckily there wasn't. The stove soaked up a lot of the blast as well, so you got singed instead of scattered. Sorry."

"I'm not." I looked at Honey. "I did something to step on somebody's toes. And the only thing I've been doing lately is talking about TPD."

Lincoln made a sound and I looked over at him. "You're not starting that shit again are you?" he asked.

"I never stopped," I said.

He shook his head, took one last look at Honey, and left the room.

"Honey, how'd you like to take the kids and get the hell out of Dodge?" I asked.

"The kids are at Chuck's mother's house now. They'll stay there for a while. It's not far from the schools and Leonard can take the younger ones in his car. He'll bitch about it, but he'll live."

"That may be too close," I said.

"You wanna move the kids on up to Oklahoma, go on ahead. Though they won't be real happy about being that far from their mama. But I'm staying put."

I closed my eyes and tried not to say anything about womanhood and the stubbornness of the breed. I didn't feel like getting hit on my scorched flesh.

"How's Jewel doing?" I finally asked.

Honey shook her head. "She won't talk. She just lies there staring at the ceiling. She's taking Henry's death real hard."

"Has she said any more about Henry's visitor?"

"Not a word."

"Does she know she's being accused?"

Honey lowered her head, not meeting my eyes. "Honey? Does she know? Tell me."

Honey sighed. "That asshole Lincoln came into her room this afternoon. I was with her. He read her her fucking rights!" And Honey burst into tears.

I patted her hand, leaving it streaked with the clear antiseptic goop. "What's his plan?"

She gulped in air and said, "She's under house arrest. Round the clock guard at the door. As soon as Hussain says she's ready to be moved, they're moving her to the county mail infirmary."

I shook my head. "No, they're not," I said. "Get me Dr. Hussain and tell Chuck it's time to call that lawyer of his."

Honey looked at me, a spark of life in her eyes, and scurried from the room. In a minute, the harried doctor returned with her.

"Dr. Hussain," I said, "I hate to tell you this, but I'm pretty sure my sister is going to have a relapse."

The doctor knitted his brows for a moment, then his face relaxed in a smile, and he said something to the effect that it was a real shame the lady was still so sick and it didn't look like she could be moved for quite a while. I distinctly heard the word "Complications." He and I smiled at each other and Honey hugged him, which he seemed to enjoy a great deal. I didn't blame him.

After the doctor had left the room, I tried to get up but Honey wasn't having any of it. When I explained what I wanted to do, she said "Only in a wheelchair." So she went down the hall and came back with one and helped me into it and then wheeled me down the hall to Jewel's room.

She was lying there just like Honey had said, staring at the ceiling glassy-eyed. We would never have gotten in the room, past the guard, if Honey hadn't sweet-talked us in—as acid-tongued as the lady could be, she could certainly earn her name when she wanted to.

Honey closed the door behind us and wheeled me next to Jewel's bed. Jewel didn't even glance at us as we entered. I leaned across the bed and took her head gently in my hands and moved it to force her focus onto me. She stared at me, but she wasn't real happy about it.

"We gotta talk, Jewel," I said.

She didn't say a word, didn't nod her head or stick out her tongue or anything. She just stared.

"Right after you came out of the coma, you said Henry had had a visitor when you got back that Friday night. You remember saying that, Jewel?"

She just stared and for a minute I thought maybe me saying to the doctor that she'd had a relapse hadn't been just a ploy. But then she moved her head out of my hand and started staring at the ceiling again. And she spoke. She said, "Leave me alone."

I took her head in my hands again, this time not as gently. "I'm not leaving you alone. Your kids' futures depend on what you can tell me, Jewel. So we're gonna talk. If not for your sake, at least for theirs."

She tried to pull out of my grasp again but I held tight. Honey tried to pull my hand off of her, saying, "You're hurting her," but I wouldn't let go.

"I'll slap her silly if I have to," I told Honey, not taking my eyes off my sister, "but I'm getting at the truth."

"I don't remember!" Jewel shouted and then began to cry. I let go of her face and Honey pushed me aside and held on to her friend, stroking her hair and letting Jewel wet her shoulder.

After about half a minute, I pushed Honey aside. "That's enough. Now business."

Jewel glared at me but Honey backed off, knowing we had to do it.

"I said I don't remember!"

"Well, try, goddamnit!" I shouted back.

"Go away! Why are you here? I don't want you here! I hate your guts! I always have! Now go away!"

I grabbed her face in my hands again and held on. "I'm not going away and there's nothing you can do to make me. I'm going to keep you out of jail, little girl, whether you want me to or not. Now, what's the last thing you can remember?"

I'd loosened my grip on her face and she moved it to the ceiling again. I reached for it and she swatted at me with her hand. "Don't do that!"

"Then talk to me or you're gonna have both your cheeks bruised!"

She sighed and looked at me and if looks could kill, I'd be six feet under with pancake makeup on my face, playing footsy with Henry.

"I don't remember anything," she said.

"It was a Friday. The kids came home from school..."

"Yes. They came home."

"There was gonna be a basketball game that night..."

"Yes."

"Henry came home from work and you all had dinner..."

She shook her head. "No. I had dinner with the kids. Henry was late. Leonard drove the VW and took Marlene and Carl with him to the high school."

"When did Henry get home?"

She shook her head again. "I don't know. I had to go to the store. We were out of bread and milk. I don't do my shopping until Saturday. But we were low. So I went to the store."

"And when you got home?"

She shook her head again. "I don't remember."

I grabbed her cheeks again and said, "Yes, you do!"

She pulled away from me and glared. "Henry was home."

"Alone?" I asked.

"No."

"Who was with him?"

Again, she shook her head. "I don't know."

I reached for her cheeks and she pulled away. "Really, Milton! I don't know who it was! A man! I'd never seen him before! I don't know who it was."

"What were they doing?"

"Nothing."

"What do you mean, nothing?"

She shrugged. "They weren't doing anything! Henry was standing in the den, the man...the man had his back to me...Henry saw me and started to say something to me...the man...the man turned around and saw me..."

She stopped and Honey moved to the other side of the bed and sat on it, putting her arms around Jewel.

"Say it, Jewel," she said quietly. "Tell Milton what happened. You've got to."

Jewel looked up at Honey and I could see tears in her eyes. Slowly, she nodded her head and turned back to me.

"There was something in his hand. Maybe a gun. I don't know. I think now, now that I know Henry was killed, it must have been a gun, but I don't remember thinking that...that it was a gun, you know, at the time." She shook her head.

"He moved toward me, fast. And Henry grabbed his arm. The one with the gun, or whatever it was. And ... and ... the man ... turned to Henry ..." she began sobbing, "and Henry ... he yelled to me ... he yelled, 'Baby, run' ... like that ... 'Baby, run' ... but I didn't ... I couldn't ... and I heard a noise ... maybe a gunshot, I don't know ... just a noise ... and Henry fell ... and then the man was on me ..." And Jewel broke down and began to sob against Honey's chest, with Honey stroking her hair and cooing to her. I took my sister's hand in mind and held it, not much maybe, but it was all I could think of to do.

TEN

THE NEXT MORNING I was released and Honey came to the hospital to pick me up. I'd noticed something strange outside my window that morning but really hadn't paid much attention to it, but once outside the hospital I couldn't help but pay attention and try to figure out what the hell it was. Then it dawned on me. Sunshine. The temperature must have been somewhere in the mid-seventies, the sun was shining and, I swear to God, Houston looked almost pretty. There were birds singing in the trees and I even saw a flower trying to break through the ground in a bed outside the hospital.

"God, what a beautiful day," I said for want of anything more poetic to pop into my head.

"Yeah, but this is dangerous," Honey said.

"Dangerous?"

"Yep. This is the kinda day when a snowbird flies down on business, leaving behind the muck and yuck of Detroit or some other nasty old place, sees this, wires the wife, 'Sell the house and pack up!' Six months later this same idiot dies of heat prostration trying to play nine holes of golf in the middle of August. Assholes.''

"Snowbirds, huh? Get a lot of 'em?"

"I saw a bumper sticker the other day that said, 'Last one out of Michigan, turn off the lights!' Before the shit hit the fan, you used to see more Michigan license tags than Texas tags and I'm only exaggerating a little bit.''

We piled my stuff in her car and she said, "With it being such a pretty day, how'd you like to see a pretty part of Houston first?"

"There's a pretty part of Houston?"

She didn't hit me. Only because she didn't wanna get the goop on her, I suppose.

We left the hospital district and got on one freeway, then moved to another that went right by that other downtown. Very confusing city. Not far from the other downtown, she pulled off the freeway on a street called Memorial Drive and after about a minute, we were in the middle of a forest of pine trees. She pulled off the road and stopped the engine. Without saying a word, we got out of the car and began to walk the trails, deep into the heart of the forest.

After a while, we stopped and I looked up at the pines towering above me, listening to the birds sing, and felt the soft breeze blowing. And I tried to pretend I was somewhere far away, in a forest in the piney woods, but I couldn't. And I didn't know why. It took me a minute before I realized that the reason I couldn't was that Godawful hum. That city hum that penetrated even into this beautiful sanctuary. You couldn't escape that hum, not in the middle of the night or in the middle of a forest. The city forever let you know it was there. It had no pulse, no rhythm, just a constant, irritating hum.

We left and Honey took me back to her house, where she'd set up the guest room as a sick room. I had my own private bottle of the antiseptic goop and the pain wasn't too bad, but my scalp and forehead, where the eyebrows used to be, itched like the very devil.

The night before I'd had Jewel describe the man to me. The man who'd been in the house with Henry.

"He was a Mexican, I think," she'd said. "Dark. Dark hair and eyes, olive complexion, dark mustache. Hooked nose. About thirty, maybe a little younger. About Henry's height, but stockier," is what she'd described. And I lay in bed in Honey's guest room thinking how her description could fit somebody from the Middle East just as much as Mexico, and how there was oil in the Middle East and how Henry had worked for an oil company and how big business sometimes got into things not quite kosher, and how maybe Mr. Durang from TPD might be into some fancy finagling with the OPEC nations and had sent an Arab hit man to off my brother-in-law for reason or reasons unknown.

Then I thought maybe the clear-colored antiseptic goop was doing things to my brain. Then I thought as how I'd heard a lot in my life about hot-tempered Latin lovers and maybe Henry'd been messing with this guy's lady. Then I thought maybe I'd like to take a nap.

That afternoon, I called Elberry Blankenship and told him what was happening.

"Now ain't that interesting?" he said.

"I thought you might find it so, Sheriff."

"So what do the cops think?"

"That Jewel Anne got out of bed, dragging her intravenous bottle behind her, and got her a couple of quick lessons in engineering, and blew up her big brother."

"Now, Milton..."

"I don't know what they think, Elberry, but they sure as hell haven't changed their minds any as far as I can tell."

"Who's in charge of that case down there?"

I gave him David Lincoln's name and number, and while he was in a writing frame of mind, gave him Honey's address. Then I asked what I called to ask.

"Sheriff, how come I got a paycheck last week? According to my records, my sick leave and vacation shoulda run out by now."

"Well, it's a new county policy..."

"What policy's that, Sheriff?"

"Well, it's not so much a policy, I guess you'd say, as, well..."

It took some doing, but I managed to get him to confess that the last check had come out of his own pocket.

Life's a funny little puppy sometimes, ya know? I'd known and worked for the Sheriff for eighteen years and knew him to be hard as nails, even though usually a fair man. I knew that he'd give you the time of day if you'd asked him proper, but I never knew him to give away money. Or even loan it. I was touched. Then I asked him how much interest.

Before we rang off, he said, "By the way, we need you back here quick. We got us a real crime wave on our hands."

"What's that, Sheriff?"

"The Bishop Shop 'N' Save got hit."

"What they take?"

"Guess."

"A case of peaches?"

"Three cases of peaches."

We both laughed and hung up. The Bishop Shop 'N' Save would make the fourth store in the county to get hit in a year. All in all, there was now something like a total of ten cases of peaches missing. Some day when it's all over, I'm gonna write a book, *The Case of the Pilfered Peaches*.

Then I got to thinking about home, and I knew I'd have to wind this up real soon. I had a life I had to get back to. But I couldn't leave with my sister in jail for a crime she didn't commit. If I lost my house on Mountain Falls Road, well, I guess I could live with that. If I lost my job, I could live with that too. What I couldn't live with would be my baby sister in jail. I couldn't die with it either, because if God saw fit to send me to Heaven, I'd no doubt meet up with Mama and Daddy and have some heavy explaining to do.

While I was laying there in Honey's guest room, she came in with the cordless phone to tell me I had a call. She didn't look real pleased about it. I picked up the phone and heard Lisa's voice.

"Milt? Are you okay?"

"'Bout as well as could be expected, Lisa. Thank you."

"I heard about it on the news! My God, what happened?"

So I explained, embellishing it a little for effect.

"Well, I'm coming right over to see you!" she said.

"Well, now Lisa, you think that's a good idea? I'm not at my sister's place anymore. I'm staying at a friend's. The lady you met . . ."

"Now, Milton, you just tell her to go polish the goldfish, 'cause a real woman's coming over to play." And she hung up.

I didn't think Honey was going to take too kindly to Lisa visiting. When I told her we had company coming, she remembered some shopping she had to do.

I was married for a very long time, and early on in that marriage I'd tried talking the wife into something the guys had all been bragging about. She tried once, told me it was the most disgusting thing in the world, and swore if I ever even asked her to do that again, she'd divorce me in a New York minute. But these modern city girls must feel a bit differently about that, and if you think about it, it was right considerate of Lisa, what with my busted rib, the hole in my cheek, and my singed flesh. Hell, I didn't even muss my hair, what's left of it. Yeah, Lisa was a very considerate lady, all in all.

I'd never been much of what you'd call a sexual athlete, but I was definitely learning some new tricks. I wondered idly about trying some of this stuff with Glenda Sue when and if I ever got home, then thought maybe she might want to know where I learned it. And then I felt guilty for even thinking about Glenda Sue when I was doing strange things with another woman. Then I felt guilty about doing strange things with another woman. Then I thought, what the hell, and pushed it all from my mind. I felt damned good when she left.

When Honey came home from the store she acted normal enough, but when she served liver for dinner, I knew she was getting some of her own back. Which I still didn't understand fully. She had Chuck, why couldn't I have Lisa? Answer that one for me, will ya?

The kids made it over for dinner and we all sat around trying to figure out who tried to blow me up. Marlene was the nicest about my injuries and wanted to put my goop on for me. I declined the offer.

The consensus of the whole group, Chuck, Honey, the kids, and me, was that me getting blown up obviously had something to do with Henry getting killed.

Carl's theory was that it was Iranian terrorists. His details were sketchy but his theory was firm. Marlene figured they had the wrong house, 'cause who in the world would want to shoot her daddy, the nicest man in the world? Leonard was very quiet. Lately, it seemed, he'd been doing that a lot. Namely, nothing. Most of his dinner was left untouched on his plate. But I didn't know Leonard well enough to know if this was normal behavior. All I knew was that when I was sixteen years old, I ate everything on my plate and anybody else's plate I could get my hands on. Truth be known, I still do. But that's another story.

We didn't discuss the possibility of Henry's women in front of the children, but I did get into my TPD theory. Carl and Marlene seemed to think about as much of it as Honey. Strangely enough, though, Chuck went for it. Which made me do a little rethinking on it. If Chuck liked it, I was probably wrong. I wasn't watching Leonard. I wasn't looking at him. Maybe I should have been.

When I mentioned what Jewel had said in the hospital, describing the assailant and how that could fit an Arab as well as a Mexican, Leonard got up and left the table. Honey and Chuck and I looked at each other, but we didn't follow him to see what was the matter. None of us were parents. Maybe a parent would have known.

Meanwhile, my sister was under house arrest in her hospital bed, waiting to get well enough to go to jail. I figured if she'd known that when she was in a coma, she'd still be there. Going to jail's no great incentive toward healing.

The next day was a Saturday and Chuck and Leonard and I spent it in Jewel's house, boarding up windows and cleaning up crud. The kitchen was a minor disaster. Chuck said that, eventually, the homeowner's insurance would take care of the repairs. But, since the case was under investigation by the arson unit of the fire department, the insurance company wouldn't do anything until the arson unit had finished and given them their findings. I said, wonderful. That's all I needed.

Things went well, for the most part. Except when Leonard threw a mostly burned pot through what was left of the kitchen window. Chuck and I just looked at each other and didn't say much. The boy went out into the yard and picked up the pot so we let it go. What did either of us know? We weren't parents.

On Monday, I had a moving company come and pack up all of Jewel's things, except those that the kids needed, and had them put in storage. And the kids and I moved into Honey and Chuck's house on a semi-permanent basis.

Living in Honey's house wasn't much harder than just seeing her every day, which I'd been doing anyway. I was a big boy, I figured I could handle it. The boys stayed in the guest room with me, on mattresses of Jewel's we didn't put in storage, and Marlene slept in Chuck's study on the hideaway couch. And Jewel slept in her hospital bed under guard. It wasn't the happiest of times.

That first night, Carl went to sleep pretty easily, although he wanted to make a slumber party out of it, I think. But Leonard just went and laid down on his mattress pretty as you please with not a peep out of him. He just turned his head and stared at the wall. When I woke up to pee around three o'clock in the morning, he was still staring at the wall.

"Leonard?" I said.

He turned his head slightly but his eyes never met mine.

"Yeah?"

"What are you doing up, boy? It's late."

He shrugged. "Can't sleep."

I crawled over to his mattress trying hard not to walk on Carl's and wake him up. "You wanna talk?" I asked.

He shook his head. "'Night," he said, and closed his eyes.

The next day we found out that living in Chuck's house, you had to play by Chuck's rules, which meant the grand tour of his toys. And the boy had some toys, I gotta tell ya. In the garage, put up for winter, was his ski boat, an eighteen-foot inboard Ski Natique with a silver metallic paint job, and his jet ski, windsurfer, and about $1,000 worth of deep-sea fishing gear. There was also a motorcycle, a ten-speed bike, and a sailplane. The cars, of course, had permanent homes in the driveway.

Inside the house, there was every gadget known to mankind, including his Ronco collection.

"Gonna be worth some money one of these days," he informed me proudly, showing off his Dice & Slice, Pocket Fisherman, and other such. And electronics I hadn't seen outside a shopping mall.

His proudest possession was a computer that the Pentagon would have been happy to call their own. In the living room alone there were two TVs with four VCRs, one of which let you get a four-way split screen so you could confuse yourself totally.

And the telephones—everything from Kermit the Frog holding the receiver in his little green hand to a combination telephone/clock radio with a keyboard where you could punch in somebody's name and the phone would dial itself. I swear to God! Every room, including the bathrooms, had a telephone and a TV, some of the TVs so tiny you had to have a magnifying glass to see what show you were watching. I'm telling you, the boy liked his toys.

One bad thing about living in the same house as Honey, she knew whenever I got a call from Lisa and whenever I left she suspected where I was going. More often than not, she was right. I can't say I knew Lisa any better than the night I'd met her, because talking was something we seldom did, if you know what I mean. But that week, the week we all moved in with Honey and Chuck, I found out by accident something about Lisa.

It was on the Wednesday. Chuck was at a Jay-Cee's meeting and Honey and the kids and I were watching TV when I got the call.

"You coming over?" she asked.

"Didn't know I'd been invited."

"Well, I'm off and I'm horny."

Now, how's that for an invitation? I asked Honey if she minded watching the kids while I went out for a bit and she just glared at me, which I took to mean okay. Why look for trouble, you know? So I drove Jewel's car over to Lisa's place.

We were in the middle of what you might call foreplay, curled up in the dry bathtub. Something new she wanted to try. The bathtub was one of those old clawfooted types and I remarked on it. "Haven't seen one of these since I was a little boy," I said.

"They had these kind when you were a kid?" she asked.

"Well, they weren't exactly modern then, but yeah, they were around."

She snuggled up close to me. "So tell me about the olden days," she said.

"I'm not that old, girl."

She grinned. "Yeah, you are. What, fifty?"

I pulled in my gut a little. "Not quite."

"Forty-nine?"

"Sorta."

"That'd make you" —she played with her fingers for a minute—"'bout thirty years older than me. I could be the daughter you had late in life."

I pulled away a little. "Your fingers aren't adding up right, Lisa. How old are you? Late twenties, right?"

She straddled me, her naked body pressing against mine. "I turned twenty last week."

It's amazing the strength you have you don't even know about. I lifted that little girl up and deposited her on the floor by the tub. Then got out, got dressed, and left. The phone rang as I opened the door to leave. As I was closing it, I heard her say, "Sure, baby, come on over. Nobody here but us chickens." Yeah, she was chicken little and I was chicken shit.

Thinking she was in her late twenties, I felt even then like a dirty old man. With my new knowledge, all I could do was say, "Bye, nice knowing you." And go home to Honey and Chuck's house and feel like a child molester.

It was only about nine o'clock when I got back to the house. The kids were off in their appointed rooms doing their homework or keeping themselves otherwise occupied, and Honey was staring at the TV. I sat down and stared with her.

Next October I'm going to be fifty years old. Half a century. And here I'd been messing with a child nearly thirty years younger than me. I was going bald by the time she was born. I had my first ulcer while she was still nibbling on her Zweiback. When she was in the first grade, I'd gotten my promotion to head deputy and had a house of my own. When you think about it that way, it sure makes a difference. It sure makes you feel dirty. Being seduced, I decided, wasn't all it's cracked up to be. But I also decided I didn't like the way I'd left it.

Just walking out the way I'd done. I've never been proud of some of the cowardly ways I have, specially with women. I figured maybe I'd better do something about that. Like say a formal good-bye. But not at her place. No way. I thought maybe I'd drop by the After Hours again.

At ten o'clock on the dot, Honey picked up the remote control, turned off the TV, stood up, and started to march out of the room. She hadn't spoken to me since I'd walked in the door.

"Honey, you wanna sit down a minute?" I asked.

I could see her back sigh even though I couldn't hear it. Slowly, she turned around. "Why?"

"Because you're mad at me and I'd like to find out why."

"Mad at you? Whatever in the world makes you think I'm mad at you?"

The stuff she's called after was dripping off her tongue.

"The way you're acting, for one thing," I said. "Now, come on, sit down here with me and let's talk."

"I have things to do."

"Like what?"

"Like wash my hair. And I have some unmentionables soaking in the sink that need to be rinsed out before Chuck gets home. I really don't have the time, Milton."

"I won't be seeing Lisa anymore."

"That really isn't any of my business."

"You're right," I said, "it's not. But I thought I'd just pass it on anyway."

She didn't smile. I know she wanted to but she didn't. She just said, "Good night," and turned and left the room.

I sat there for a while staring at the blank TV screen, then finally got up and took my shower. As I was coming out, I heard the front door opening and went to greet Chuck.

"Hey, man," I said, "How was your meeting?"

"Boring as shit. How was your evening?"

"Strange. These things get out pretty late, huh?"

"What the fuck's that supposed to mean?"

"Nothing. Just conversation. Sorry."

"You sound worse than Honey."

I excused myself and went to the guest room and crawled into bed.

The next day, around noon, to save Honey from having to fix me lunch, I went over to the After Hours. Al was behind the bar, rubbing what looked like the same glass with what looked like the same rag. I thought, at that moment, that maybe when I retired, I'd open me up a bar in Longbranch. Didn't seem to be such a hard life.

"Hey, Al," I called.

"Hey, yourself. What happened to you?"

"What? Oh." I remembered how I must look to the outside world, with no eyebrows and lashes, and my pretty pink skin. "Little home accident."

"Thought maybe you were going for the bald look like me and shaved the wrong part of your head!" He laughed that booming laugh of his and I smiled.

"Got a light beer?" I asked.

"Miller, right?"

"You got a good memory."

"Gotta have in this business."

"Lisa around?"

"Naw, won't get in till around five."

"Oh." I decided to leave a note instead. Didn't see any use in hanging around half the day to say, "Sorry, kid." "You got some paper I can write on?" I asked Al.

"Sure. Just a minute."

He pulled out a pad of writing paper with the logo of an oil rigging company and handed me a piece. I wrote, "Lisa—Sorry about the other night. But the age thing really got to me. I'm too old for new tricks. Thanks. Bye." And I signed it "Milt."

So maybe nobody's ever gonna collect my letters for posthumous publication, but it was certainly to the point.

I drained the beer, folded the paper, put Lisa's name on the outside, and handed it to Al.

"Give this to Lisa when she comes in?" I asked.

He took the paper and put it in the till, under the money tray. "Sure, no problem."

I left some change on the counter and took off.

That had been on Thursday, when I left the note for Lisa, and on Friday, Chuck decided his car needed a tune-up.

"Baby, you take it by Sid's for me? See what the fuck he can do? It knocks all the fuckin' time."

So Chuck took Honey's car, the kids left for school, and Honey made an appointment with Sid to fix Chuck's Porsche.

When we were ready to go, me to follow in Jewel's car to bring Honey home, she directed me to the big plate-glass window in the living room that had a view of the driveway and Chuck's Porsche. "Watch this," she said. In her hand was a remote-control unit.

"You wanna watch TV?" I asked, my coat already on.

"Nope. This is one of the few toys of Chuck's I like." She pushed a button on the control and we stood by the window and watched Chuck's Porsche blow up.

It all sorta happened in slow motion. Like watching an instant replay of a Cowboys' game on TV. The car burst into flames and the concussion from the blast swelled the plate-glass window we were standing in front of. The swell exploded, knocking Honey and me down amidst a shower of broken glass. Somehow I managed to shield my face and push Honey behind me before we were knocked down. Shards of glass went into my back and Honey's legs.

"Seems an expensive way to have fun to me," I managed to say, once the glass had stopped flying.

"It's not supposed to do that," Honey said, watching the flames shooting up in the driveway.

"Lay on your stomach," I said.

"Don't get kinky on me, Milton, it's not the time or place."

"Don't get any cuter than you already are, woman. You got glass in your back side. And so do I. I'll do you and you do me."

She giggled. "Just don't tell Chuck."

I started as gently as possible to extract the shards. "How can you flirt at a time like this?" I asked.

"Just comes natural, I sup—" The word turned into a yelp of pain as I pulled out the glass.

She got mine out none too gently and I excused myself and ran to the phone to call the fire department. I figured one more time, and they'd start charging us. I also figured we'd wait to mend our wounds till after we took care of the hullabaloo outside.

By the time we got in the yard, half the neighborhood, which consisted of two housewives and five unemployed engineers, was standing in the street staring at the damage. The grass was burning in the yard near the Porsche and Honey and I began stomping on it to put it out. The neighbors finally joined in and we kept it from spreading before the fire trucks arrived.

I noticed Honey's plate-glass window wasn't the only one broken. The people across the street were gonna be surprised when they got home.

While the fire department was doing their thing, I called Sergeant Lincoln. I knew when the arson squad showed up what they'd find. Lincoln, for a change, decided that the whole thing was mighty interesting.

Before he came over, I suppose he called the hospital to make sure my sister was still in her room under guard and hadn't been sneaking out in the cold to blow up her best friend's car, being the homicidal maniac she is. And finally, when he got to Honey's house, he was willing to think that maybe Henry being killed, Jewel being shot, me being blown up with the gas stove, and Chuck's car going bang might be connected and might not have anything to do with Jewel. I had to give the boy some credit, I know it's hard admitting you're wrong.

"What about them Asians that beat me up?" I asked, trying my best to get everything into one big package.

"What about 'em?" Lincoln asked.

"I still think that's connected. You've heard of the Yakusa, right?"

He sighed and ignored me. And then, of course, he did diddle with the theory that Honey and I were having a passionate affair and Chuck blew up the stove and put a bomb in his own car for his wife. But Honey put him off that one in a hurry by making a slight threat to his manhood.

So he and Honey and I sat down and Honey and I told him everything we'd found out; everyone we'd interviewed, everything Jewel had remembered about that night, and everywhere we'd gone since the whole thing started.

And he said, "It's gotta be a jealous boy-friend."

"What about TPD?" I asked.

He sighed and Honey sighed and I got pissed. It was as good a theory as anybody else's.

"TPD is a rock-solid company, Milt. After you said it the first time, I checked into them. They're owned by three people, Nelson Durang, Paul Peabody, and the widow of Albert Turner. Durang has a fifty-one percent controlling interest. He moved the company into computers at the insistence of your brother-in-law ten years ago, before the shit hit the fan and before home computers were the rage. Now he's doing better with computers than he ever did in oil. Even in the good old days. Nothing shady at all that I can see, and I looked hard, Milt, I really did. So drop it, okay?"

"How much stock you got in TPD?" I asked, not one to let go of an idea with what you might call a smidgen of grace.

Lincoln laughed. "Not a public company, Milt, or I'd sell my wife's left tittie to get in—excuse me, Miz Lancaster."

"So now what?" I asked.

"So now we look into Henry's sex life a little bit more."

And he left. I heard the back door open and Chuck came in and threw himself on the sofa, lengthwise. "I fuckin' don't believe this shit," he said. I'd never seen him so depressed and it worried me.

"You okay?" I asked.

He shook his head. "What the fuck's going on, Milt? Huh? What the fuck's going on?"

"I wish I knew, I really do."

He lifted his head up and turned to look at me. "Somebody's trying to kill me now? Is that it? Or were they after Honey? Or you? What?"

I shook my head. I didn't know. "I loved that little car, Milt," he said with a sigh. "It was a fuckin' bullet, my little car. That car added a whole fuckin' inch to my pecker, ya know?"

I nodded my head. "That car made me look fuckin' *good*, ya know?"

Again I nodded. He sighed and lay back, staring at the ceiling. The car had been a Porsche, a '78 Porsche, and I knew what he meant. Back home in Longbranch, I have a '55 Chevy hardtop. In cherry condition. I knew how I'd feel if somebody blew up my baby. But what can you say? I left Chuck to his depression and went in to help Honey with dinner and try to explain to the kids what was happening.

And try not to think about the fact that Chuck seemed more worried about this car than his wife and me. Of course, Honey and I would heal. The Porsche wouldn't.

Two days later, Lincoln got back to me. And he found out what I'd found out, that Henry's ladies didn't expect anything more out of Henry than a real good lay, which they all claimed is exactly what they got. None of them had a jealous lover or boyfriend, they claimed, and they all swore that to their knowledge Henry had never dated married women. I didn't tell Lincoln I told him so, which I figured showed a heap of restraint on my part.

And we were right back to square one.

"You still plan on indicting my sister?" I asked, sitting on Honey's living room with the sergeant.

"That'll be up to the DA's office. I'll let them know what's been going on. It's their call."

"Well, you tell 'em, David, that it's obvious Jewel didn't do this. There's more going on than that and you know it. You tell 'em I want to get my sister and her kids outta here and back to Oklahoma soon as I can. You tell 'em that, okay?"

We both stood up and shook hands and Lincoln said, "I'll do that, Milt. I don't see how she did this either, if you wanna know the truth."

I figured maybe that wasn't much, him saying that, but like Chuck would say, Fuck it, it was something.

ELEVEN

"I MOVED Evinrude in with me," Glenda Sue said, "'cause he said he was lonely in that big old house all by himself. Besides, keeps me from having to drive up there more than once a week."

"You still watering the plant?"

"Why else would I go up there once a week?"

"How's Muffy like Evinrude living with you?" Muffy was Glenda Sue's Great Dane bitch.

Glenda Sue laughed. "I gotta tell you, Milt, that's one weird cat you got there. He's been coming on to Muffy since he moved in. She's pretty nervous about it."

I laughed too. "Well, if he has his way with her, take pictures okay?"

"You're sick, Kovak."

"Yeah, but you said that's what you liked about me."

"Enough. How's Jewel?"

"Depressed. How else would she be? Now that the Grim Reaper's not hanging over her bed, the police are."

"That's just plain stupid. Don't they know she would never do anything like that?"

"No, honey, I'm afraid they don't."

"Why don't you send the kids on up here to me? I'll take care of them while you finish what you have to do."

I thought about it for a moment. "Maybe later. Right now, I think they need to be near their mama. And I know Jewel needs 'em around. They're all she's got right now."

"Milt, if you need me for anything..."

"Honey, you're doing plenty just keeping my life together up there."

"Hey."

"What?"

"Funniest thing..."

"What's that?"

"I miss you."

I grinned. "Yeah? Well, that's good. Because I miss you too."

"Good."

"Well, I guess I'd better hang up."

"Yeah, I gotta go feed the beasts. Call me."

"Yeah. Bye."

I hung up and lay on the bed staring at the ceiling and feeling a little guilty about humping a child like Lisa when I had a lady like Glenda Sue waiting

for me back home. I was a lucky man. And Glenda
Sue was a fine woman. Always had been. And what
basically was the difference between me screwing
around on a lady like Glenda Sue, even if she wasn't
my wife, and Henry screwing around on Jewel?
Just a piece of paper, that's all the difference there
was.

I didn't tell Glenda Sue about either explosion.
Why worry her? She would have insisted on the
kids moving up there to stay with her, which probably would be best, but then what would Jewel
have? Just me. That had never been much before
and I doubt if it was now, even if she did smile at
me every once in a while. It was the kind of smile
you give a vacuum cleaner salesman while you're
shutting the door in his face, so I figured it didn't
mean much.

Life's a funny little puppy, ya know? All those
years of neglecting my sister, not thinking about her
very existence, content in the life the wife and I had
built, the life that had crumbled so easily and so
completely the day she walked out, all those years
were coming back to haunt me. The only good
memory I had of my sister, the only loving memory in her whole thirty-five years was a memory
from before she was even born. That hardly seemed
right, but there it was. And it was a memory she

didn't even know about. One she didn't share with me. I bet if she searched her mind and her heart, she couldn't come up with one good memory of me. I lay there in the bed staring at the ceiling, and thinking that as a human being, I sucked eggs.

And as a detective, I wasn't doing a hell of a lot better. Somebody was out there and he was mighty pissed off, and I didn't know who or why. And then I decided, to steal from my friend Chuck, fuck a bunch of 'em. Tomorrow I was heading to TPD and an interview with Mr. Durang himself.

Which was weird. When I called first thing in the morning and told the receptionist and then the secretary and then the administrative assistant who I was, I got an immediate interview. That surprised me.

The head office of TPD Industries was in a high rise in the main downtown area, the real one. I showed the pedestrians on the streets of Houston just what a hick I was by almost falling down outside the building while bending over backward to stare up and see in which cloud the building ended.

The lobby was black slate floors with chrome fittings on black vinyl walls and weird red, black, and white wall hangings bigger than my house. The escalator, that took me from the ground floor to the main floor where the elevator banks were, had glass sides with chrome fittings and moved fast enough to make me just a little nervous.

The main floor was decorated in the same way and the elevator would have made a nice little condo. It was paneled in what looked like teak and had plush black carpeting and chrome and black vinyl fittings. And it just went on and on. My ears popped at the twenty-second floor and by the time we got to the thirty-fifth, where TPD had the whole floor, I was feeling about as nervous as a long-tailed cat in a room full of rocking chairs.

Walking through the glass doors to the reception area, I tried not to look out the huge floor-to-ceiling window behind the receptionist's desk. Probably a pretty view of the city, I kept telling myself, but the other part of myself kept saying, in this high squeaky voice, "Don't look down! Don't look down!"

It took three nice-looking young ladies to get me to my destination, but I finally got there. I had to sit outside in the waiting area for about five pleasant minutes staring at Durang's administrative assistant, a very pretty, very no-nonsense type in her mid-thirties with great legs. It was either stare at her or out her floor-to-ceiling window, which I didn't feel up to.

TPD's offices didn't match the rest of the building. I'd noticed that the minute I'd walked through the glass doors. The carpets were a deep blue plush, the furniture either antique or good reproductions, the appointments lavish. I felt a little underdressed in my gray slacks and gray-and-black checked jacket. I didn't have a tie. I'd brought one with me to wear to the funeral, but that's the only place I wear one. Funerals and weddings. Back home, when I wasn't wearing my uniform, which I didn't, mostly, I was supposed to wear a suit and tie. For several years now I've been trying to set a new fashion, seer-sucker suit without tie. One of these days, it's gonna catch on. It's gonna be the rage. Don Johnson beware. Milton Kovak's right behind you.

Finally, the pretty lady with the great legs got up and exposed a few extra inches of thigh to escort me into the bowels of TPD. Namely, Mr. Durang's office. I've seen bowling alleys that were smaller, I swear to God, and I guess Mr. Durang read all the propaganda about the bigger the executive, the cleaner the desk, because he didn't even have a desk. The office looked like a living room in somebody's fancy house, with more antiques sitting alongside some expensive modern-looking stuff. There was a coffee table about the size of my living room surrounded by low couches and that's where Durang was sitting when I walked in. Not sitting so much, actually, as lounging. When he stood up, I got a firm handshake, a sorrowful smile, and a pat on my back.

I'd met him before, of course, at the funeral, and he didn't look much different. Maybe an inch shorter than me, five ten or thereabouts, with gray hair that was going bald in the middle, leaving a little tuft in front around a low widow's peak. His eyes were a watery blue and his skin the kind of tan I think you get at those tanning parlors I've read about. Either that, or he spent a lot of time someplace other than rainy Houston.

"Mr. Kovak," he said, his voice low and solicitous like we were still at the funeral, "please, sit down."

I sank into the overstuffed couch and tried to look comfortable. "What can I do for you?" he asked.

"Well, Mr. Durang, I got a problem."

"Anything I can do, just tell me."

"My sister didn't kill Henry."

He clucked his tongue a few times and looked at me. "I know it's hard to understand. Mrs. Hotch-kiss didn't seem the type...but who's to say what goes on in other people's hearts and minds, Mr. Kovak?''

"There was somebody at the house when she got home from the store that Friday night, Mr. Durang. That somebody shot Henry and then shot my sister."

He frowned and looked concerned. "Really? How did you find this out?"

I wondered why he didn't immediately ask "who," but let it slide. "When my sister came out of the coma, she remembered some of it."

"Oh." He smiled sadly. "Of course, Mr. Kovak, she'd say that."

How do you tell a man that your sister doesn't lie? How do you tell somebody whose whole life involved convincing other people of things by any means possible that you were talking about a little girl raised by a lady who thought lying was two steps above incest and one step above murder? How do you convince someone that another person was incapable of deception?

You don't. Not nowadays. Not people who lie about what they had for lunch, and whether or not it was raining outside. Not somebody capable of hugging somebody one minute and taking his business away from him the next. Not only does a person like that think a person like Jewel doesn't exist, but, if you convinced him she did, he'd advise you to have her put away someplace where she wouldn't hurt anybody. Because, let's face it, honesty rarely makes a buck.

"Far as I can tell, Mr. Durang," I said, "there's no reason for Jewel to have killed Henry."

Again the sad smile and the clucking of the tongue. "The oldest reason in the world, jealousy. Let's face it, Mr. Kovak, may I call you Milt? Your brother-in-law wasn't the most faithful of husbands."

I didn't feel like getting into that again, so instead I asked, "Just what was it Henry did for you, Mr. Durang?"

"Well, Milt, Henry was my accountant. Personally and the head accountant for the corporation. He was my right arm." The frown, the shake of the head. "I cannot express to you how much I miss him, both personally and professionally."

"The man who shot him, according to my sister, was an Arab." I thought I'd just sorta run that up the old flagpole and see who saluted, put it in the pipe and see how it smoked....

"Really? I wonder why."

"Why what?"

"Why she decided to say he was an Arab?"

"You're in the oil business, Mr. Durang, why don't you tell me?"

And then he laughed. A real belly laugh. The first natural sounding thing to come out of him since I walked in the room.

Finally, he stopped and looked at me and I gotta say there was what you might call amusement written all over his face. "My God, Milt, you are reaching, aren't you?"

He stood up and indicated that I do the same then led me by the arm to the door. Once there he patted my shoulder and said, "I understand what you're trying to do. And I feel for you. She's your sister. But don't fuck with me, Kovak."

He opened the door, shook my hand, and closed the door behind me.

I drove on back to Honey's and told her in detail what had transpired with Mr. TPD.

"Hmm," she said.

"Hmm? What the hell does that mean? Doesn't this burn your liver? Can't you see this man is hiding something? I know in my gut he had something to do with Henry's death..."

"Shh..." I looked up to where she was looking. At Leonard standing in the doorway.

"Hey, boy," I called, "what you doing home from school so early?"

But he didn't answer me. He just walked to his room.

That night at dinner, Leonard didn't join us. I went into the room he and Carl and I shared and found him just lying there, staring up at the ceiling.

"You gonna come eat?"

"Not hungry."

"You're skinny enough, boy. You gotta eat."

"I don't have to fucking eat if I don't want to!" It was a shout. Loud enough for the rest of them to hear it in the dining room.

"What's bothering you, son?" I asked, all solicitous like.

"I'm not your son. I'm barely your nephew."

What could I do? I turned around and went back to the dining room and stuffed my face.

The other two kids watched TV after dinner while Honey did the bills and Chuck and I did some serious beer drinking. Around ten o'clock I herded the kids to bed, Marlene to her room and Carl with me to the dormitory we shared with Leonard. He wasn't there.

At first I didn't think much of it, figuring he was in the bathroom. But when Carl got up to go to the bathroom and I heard no ruckus coming from that direction, the usual kinda thing when two siblings are sharing a confined space, I wondered. When the youngest came back, I asked him.

"Leonard in there?"

"In where?"

"The bathroom."

"Nope."

"Where is he?"

"I dunno."

"Have you seen him?"

"Not since before dinner. He was in a pi—a bad mood."

I left the room and went to Marlene's.

"You seen Leonard?"

She looked up from a teenage romance she was reading in lieu of doing homework.

"No."

I made the rounds of the whole house, including the garage, finding no Leonard. Finally, I went to the one room I had never been in. I knocked loudly on Chuck and Honey's bedroom door. Honey opened it, and I barely noticed the nightgown she was wearing.

"What is it, Milt?"

"You seen Leonard?"

"No. He's not in your room?"

"Would I ask if he was?"

"Jesus, don't get snippy with me, okay? Where is he?"

"If I knew would I be asking... right, snippy again, huh?"

"Exceedingly so." She turned her head toward the bedroom. "Chuck, have you seen Leonard?"

I heard Chuck's disembodied voice say, "No. Fuck, what's going on now?"

I heard the bed creak and the door opened wider to reveal Chuck in a pair of skivvies. A humbling experience.

"I can't find him," I told them both. "I've checked the whole house."

"You look outside?" Chuck asked.

"Not yet. But you've got the burglar alarm on, don't you?"

"Yeah. But maybe he turned it off."

He pulled on a pair of jeans and we went into the entry hall where the burglar alarm was flashing red, letting us know it was indeed working.

"When'd you turn it on?" I asked.

"Right before we went to bed."

"God only knows when he left. But he's not in the house, that's for sure."

"Well, I'm not going outside at this time of night without some fucking protection. Hold on a minute."

I wondered idly why someone that big felt he needed protection in his own neighborhood, but let it pass, figuring "protection" was just another word for "toy" in Chuck's vocabulary. Then, of course, the thought of a bunch of small Asian men standing right outside the door holding my nephew hostage slipped quietly in and out of what's left of my mind.

Chuck went down the hall to the master bedroom and I could hear him thrashing around in there. In a couple of minutes he was back.

"My gun's gone," he said.

You know that feeling you get when you're on a roller coaster and you go down that first big hill? That feeling where you left your stomach in some other place? I was standing still, but I had that feeling.

"When was the last time you saw it?" I asked, going into my policeman mode.

"Saturday. I cleaned it then."

"Leonard know where you kept it?"

Chuck sighed. "Fuck. Yeah. I showed it to him. Hell, I even showed him how to shoot it one day a while back. Him and Henry and me went out to the range and popped a few."

"Wonderful."

Chuck and I looked at each other for a long minute, both unsure what to do next.

"You notice the look on the boy's face when you were talking about Durang today?" Chuck and I both whirled around, startled, to where Honey stood staring up at us.

"Come on, Honey," I said.

"Did you see it?" she insisted.

I sighed. "Yeah, I saw it."

I turned and headed for the phone, finally getting Lincoln at his home number. I told him what I suspected and told him I'd meet him at Durang's house. Honey had the address. She and Chuck had gone there with Henry and Jewel to a party two Christmases ago. Chuck and I convinced Honey it would be best if she stayed with Carl and Marlene and Chuck pulled on a sweatshirt and he and I got in Honey's car and headed for River Oaks, the millionaires' playground of Houston.

By the time we got to the first three-story, seventy-five-room house on the block, it was almost eleven o'clock at night. I'm not exaggerating. About the three-story, seventy-five-room houses. Not the time. Well, I'm not exaggerating about the time either. But anyway, these were BIG houses. And only a couple of 'em had FOR SALE signs and none of 'em had high grass around them. I figured

even if they had been repoed, it would be worth it
to the agent handling the house to pay ten bucks a
week to some illegal to keep the lawn nice.

When we pulled up to Durang's house, I noticed
right off that all the light were on. Outdoor lights,
indoor lights, probably even the pool lights. There
was a patrol car and Sergeant Lincoln's personal
car in the driveway. We pulled up behind it and
were immediately met by a uniform.

"Can I help you gentlemen?" he asked in that
sarcastic way we learn at the academy. I call it,
"How to Piss Off the Civilians, 101."

"I'm the one who called Lincoln. My nephew
here?"

"Teenaged male with pimples and a forty-five
automatic?"

"That's him."

He let us out of the car and we followed him to
the front door of the house. As we entered, the first
thing I heard was, "This is all your fucking fault,
Kovak!"

Durang was standing in his underwear by a broken vase, or "vahse" by how much the thing probably cost. I ignored Durang, his underwear, and his
broken toy and looked around until I spotted
Leonard sitting in a straight-backed chair by the

staircase. Lincoln was standing beside him, holding the gun. I walked over to them.

"I gotta agree with Mr. Durang, Milton, you done stepped in it this time," Lincoln said. He wasn't smiling.

"Hey, Leonard," I said.

He didn't look up, just kept staring at his feet.

"Boy, look at me when I talk to you!" He did. "What did you think you were doing?" I lost him. He went back to his more interesting feet.

"Leonard, you look at those ugly, oversized feet of yours one more time, I'm gonna rip one of 'em off."

He looked up. I said, "Now. Tell me. What did you think you were doing?"

"I heard you!" he said. "I heard you tell Aunt Honey that Mr. Durang did it! He had my Daddy killed! You said it!"

Wonderful. I could feel every eye in the place staring holes in my weak back.

I knelt down next to the boy. "That was just a theory, Leonard. I've got no proof."

A half-assed sneer played around the corner of his mouth. "A forty-five doesn't need proof."

I slapped him. "You seen too damn many *Dirty Harry* movies, Leonard. Spent too much time in Rambo-ville. All killing Mr. Durang woulda got you would be a real long time in juvie and maybe even the gas chamber..."

"Lethal injection in Texas..." Chuck intervened.

"Thank you, Chuck. Lethal injection. You know what that means? They give you a shot, just like for the measles or polio, only it kills you. Dead. Like a doornail. Now's that what you want? That what you want for your mama? How in the hell do you think she'd react to that, Leonard? Jesus, boy, I didn't realize just how stupid you are!"

I turned away from him and started walking for the door. Waving my hand haphazardly behind me, I said, "Just take him away, Lincoln. He's too stupid to be my kin."

"Uncle Milt!" I noticed the whine in his voice right off the bat. That's what I'd been waiting for.

I turned. "What?"

"Don't just leave me here!"

"Why not? You shot a man, boy! They don't give you medals for that any place but in the Army, and then only if it's the right man."

"But you said—"

"I said I had a theory. And I still do. But I got other theories too. You gonna go kill everybody involved in every piss ant theory I got? Half a' Houston's in big trouble."

He sighed, long and hard. "Jesus . . ." he said.

Everybody was quiet for a minute. Everybody waiting for somebody else to do something. Finally, Lincoln broke the silence. "Mr. Durang, you wanna press charges, sir?"

I finally looked at Durang. And noticed he had a tattoo of an eagle on his left forearm. I kinda liked that. Gave him roots, you know?

Durang sighed. "Shit. No. I guess not. But you listen to me, Leonard Hotchkiss! Your daddy was a friend of mine! A good friend! And a good employee! Your daddy was so damn smart it was scary. I trusted him. He knew more about my business than I do. And I'll tell you something. I'm gonna be in trouble now that your daddy's gone. Your daddy dying didn't help me in the least. It hurt me. I'm losing money because your daddy's not here. Now why in the hell would I kill that man? Answer me that?"

Leonard, of course, didn't answer him, he just looked at me. And so did everybody else. For want of anything better to do, I said, "Mr. Durang, how much is that vase worth? Leonard will pay for it out of his allowance."

"Quarter of a million," Durang answered. Leonard went pale. Then Durang laughed. "Shit, boy, I'm just playing with you. My wife bought this at an auction in New Orleans. This and a whole box of other stuff. Paid thirty-five dollars for the whole box." In an aside to me, he said, "She's still not used to the money, still thinks we're wild-catting in west Texas." Then he straightened up, regaining what dignity he could in his underwear with his eagle in full flight. "Kovak, I gotta tell you, you are a royal pain in the ass. But this nephew of yours, he's got balls as big as his daddy's. It was your stupid idea but he's the one who put it into action. He was wrong as shit, but at least he did something. But I'm telling you now, I swear to you, on the heads of my children, I had absolutely nothing to do with Henry's death."

I walked over to Leonard and pulled him to his feet and led him and Chuck out the door.

Lincoln followed us out. After we got Leonard settled in the car with Chuck, he pulled me aside.

"You gonna stop this shit now?" he asked.

In my heart I knew my so-called oil connection was a crock. I guess I'd known it all along. And I was depressed. I guess I been reading too many conspiracy books. Watching too much television. On television, big businessmen are always crooked and not one of them would think twice about killing somebody for a buck. But that's TV. In real life, I suppose, big businessmen weren't much different than anybody else. Just richer and a little more conservative. And maybe they wouldn't bat an eye about poisoning a village in a Third World country if it meant saving $3.2 million on the construction of a plant, but I doubted if most of 'em would have a man shot. Maybe.

But I wasn't about to give Lincoln the satisfaction of saying, "I told you so." I just plain didn't answer the question. Instead, like the good cop I am, I asked a question. "What happened here anyway?"

Lincoln laughed quietly. "Leonard came through a downstairs window. Broke the glass. The alarm went off. And so did Durang's Dobermans. I'm not sure how the boy made it to the foyer without getting his ass chewed off!"

"I'll have a talk with him."

He gave me one of those looks. "Yeah. You do that."

"I said I would."

"Yeah. Right."

"Why don't you go catch you some real crooks?"

"Can't. Too busy keeping your family off the streets."

"You're a funny man."

"I try."

Figuring there was no way I was gonna get the last word, I turned and got into the car and drove off. And started thinking, which is something I seem prone to do. Can't help it. And the thoughts I had weren't good ones. They started with a fact I just couldn't get around. That fact being, I was back to square one. But I'd been back there so many times, I was thinking of getting some furniture for it. And now I had the added problem of almost turning my own nephew into a murderer.

I was beginning to feel like one of those mimes you see on TV all the time, inside the box. Trying to get out. But there was no door in this box, or no end to the circle, whichever comparison you prefer. Somebody'd killed my brother-in-law and tried to kill my sister. Why? One reason and only one came to mind.

Henry had screwed with the wrong lady. Jewel walked in and the murderer had to silence the witness. But why was he trying to kill me? Why blow up Jewel's house? Because I was getting too close? Bullshit. I was getting nowhere! Then why? Why try to kill Honey? Or were they trying for Honey? It was Chuck's car. Why try to kill Chuck?

They had to be related. There was no way these were three separate incidents. And if they were related, and they had to be, there was a clue in there somewhere. Namely, what did I have in common with Chuck? And what did Chuck have in common with Henry?

We were all men. Okay, we got a nut out there killing men. Bullshit. Okay, Henry was screwing everything in sight. He screwed the wrong lady. Chuck wasn't exactly the faithful type either. He screwed the wrong lady. But what about me? I hadn't screwed anybody but... Lisa. I'd screwed Lisa. But Henry didn't. Lisa told me that herself. But had Chuck?

I'd never mentioned the name of the lady I'd been seeing to Chuck. In some strange way it had amounted to a point of honor with me not to discuss the lady. I couldn't see Honey mentioning it either. So, was that a connection? Chuck had been to After Hours with Henry. Had he met Lisa there?

Then I remembered. The last night I'd been with Lisa, she'd gotten a phone call as I'd been leaving. And Chuck had been late getting home. A little more than twenty-four hours later, his car had been blown up.

Chuck and I needed to talk. Nothing to it but to ask him. But it would have to wait until morning. With no Leonard around, and no Honey.

Chuck was gone when I got up in the morning. Before I found him there was one thing I had to. I dug out the card the social worker had given me and called her, explaining what had happened the night before. She agreed to see Leonard that day.

"Honey?" I asked at the breakfast table. "Do me a favor?"

"Depends on what it is."

"Would you take Leonard over to see that social worker this afternoon? I think maybe the boy needs to talk about what's going on. What do you think?"

She bit into her toast and nodded her head. "Yeah. With his daddy being murdered, his mama in the hospital, and his uncle spouting off wild conspiracy theories, I guess you might say he's gotten a little confused."

"You gonna blame this whole thing on me, aren't you?"

She just smiled that cute little shit-eating grin of hers and I left, taking Jewel's car and heading over to the shopping center where Chuck's insurance agency was.

Chuck's mother was in the reception area, busily typing out invoices to Chuck's clients. The man himself saw me when I walked in the front door.

"Hey, Milt! What the fuck are you doing here?" He grinned and shook my hand as if we hadn't just seen each other the night before.

"Let's go have some lunch," I suggested.

"Fuck, man, it's only ten-thirty."

I took his arm. "Coffee, then."

With his free arm he pointed toward the Mr. Coffee machine that sat beside his desk. "We got some over here..."

I pulled and managed to get him started out the front door.

Once seated at a coffee shop down the street, with mugs of the nastiest coffee ever brewed in front of us, I asked him, "You know Lisa at After Hours?"

He grinned. "Yeah."

"You ever date her?"

He shrugged. "Well, yeah, I guess you could say that." His grin got huge. "Lisa's not exactly the type you say no to, if you get my drift."

I got his drift. About the same time I heard this little flutter by my ear, sounding like a bird in flight, right before the glassed-in case that housed the three-day-old homemade pies exploded in a million little pieces.

It seemed to take forever for my eyes to move from the shattered case to the hole an inch to the left of my head in the plate-glass window of the coffee shop, and then for them to move again to the scene outside the window. The scene of the man resting the high-powered rifle against the top of the gold Mustang and taking aim. I pushed Chuck's chair with my legs and went over backwards in my own chair as the sugar bowl on our table exploded.

"What the fuck's going on?" Chuck asked.

I looked out the broken plate glass window while yelling at the only people in the coffee shop besides us, a waitress and the cook, to get down. But the cook was having none of that. For a minute, I forgot I was in Houston. He grabbed up a sawed-off shotgun from under the cash register and hauled ass out to the sidewalk. The man with the rifle hopped into the car and took off as the cook came bursting through the doors. Red taillight glass sprinkled the pavement as the cook's shotgun went off, but the car kept going.

The man in the car had looked familiar.

Chuck, who had also been watching the scene unfold, said, "Fuck, that was Al Taylor! Why's he shooting at us?"

I jumped up and headed out the door thinking, "Yeah, why the fuck is Al Taylor, the bartender and owner of After Hours, shooting at us?"

Chuck was right behind me at the door when I turned and told the waitress to call the police, ask for Sergeant Lincoln, and to tell him what happened and to meet us at After Hours. Then Chuck and I were out the door and in the car.

TWELVE

I DON'T THINK I'd be stretching the point to say I figured I'd worn out my welcome in the fair metropolis of Houston. Hell, I didn't wanna be there in the first place. I didn't see any good reason for anybody to shoot at me to convince me to go home. I was ready. Pack my bags, I'm Oklahoma bound. Just one little ole problem keeping me back. Somebody'd killed my brother-in-law, shot my sister, beat me up, blew me up, and tried to blow me (or Chuck or Honey, who the hell knew?) up a second time. And now somebody was shooting at me and Chuck in a public place. I figured Al Taylor had some explaining to do.

We pulled up in front of the After Hours, parked the car, and got out. I looked at Chuck and he looked at me as we stood there looking at the front of the bar. We didn't see any gold Mustang in the parking lot, but as the guy owned the place, he may of parked around back.

"So what the fuck do we do now?" Chuck was whispering, which for Chuck meant that only those folks living in the immediate southwest portion of the nation could hear him enough to distinguish the words.

Being a professional peace officer, I answered, "We go inside and bust his ass is what."

Chuck's eyes got big and his one bushy eyebrow got lost somewhere in his hairline. "You got a gun, Milt?"

Boy had a point. "Well, no. But we been standing out here in plain sight of the window for the better part of a day and he hasn't shot at us yet. I figure he's either out of ammo, which ain't likely, or he ain't at home, which is more likely."

"So if he ain't the fuck there, why go in?"

Again, the boy had a point but I did have my pride. "Because that's what we're supposed to do, Chuck. We got a possible perp in there and we gotta go in. 'Sides, Lisa's probably in there and that little girl's got some explainin' to do."

"Yeah? Yeah. Suppose you're right." He looked at me and I looked at him and figured we'd stalled around long enough waiting for Lincoln to show up. With my luck, it was probably his day off. So we started for the door and for one split second I wished I had spurs on my feet so I could hear 'em jangling.

The door was locked. Being not quite eleven in the morning, After Hours was closed. Relief was mixed with a twinge of embarrassment. That's when I heard the screech of tires on pavement and turned around in time to see Sergeant Lincoln's unmarked squad car slam into the curb.

Chuck let out a long sigh. "Fuck, I almost messed my pants." He laughed a little then said, "You tell anybody that, Milt, and I'll rip you a new asshole."

"Make you a deal, Chuck. I won't tell nobody 'bout the skid marks in your pants if you don't mention the palsy I just developed all over my body."

Which may be a good time to mention that although I've been a sheriff's deputy for nearly eighteen years, I've yet had reason to even draw my gun at anybody, much less have to shoot anybody or have anybody shoot at me. Prophesy County's more or less a friendly place, not like Houston where you got bartenders trying to shoot holes in people in coffee shops.

Lincoln bailed out of his car, gun drawn. Chuck and I both held up our hands, looked at each, and burst into a fit of the giggles. Relief can do funny things to a man.

"What the shit are you two up to?" Lincoln asked, holstering his piece.

I told him what had happened and what I suspected.

"What's this guy Taylor got to do with the price of tea in China?"

"That's what me and Chuck would like to know. The only connection I can figure is . . . well, there's this girl, Lisa. She works for Al. I been out with her a few times. So's Chuck here."

Chuck beckoned Lincoln closer to him. "That's real privileged fuckin' information, Sergeant. Know what I mean?"

Lincoln gave him a dirty look and turned to me. "She one of Henry's bimbos?"

"Well, now, Dave. This is where the whole thing starts to fall apart a little bit. According to Lisa, she and Henry'd never been together at all."

"Hell. What the fuck's goin' on here?" Lincoln asked the sky. Chuck and I just shrugged. Him, me, and the sky, we sure as hell didn't know either.

Lincoln got on his car radio and asked the dispatcher to find him a home address for Al Taylor, owner and operator of the After Hours bar. While the dispatcher was getting the information, I told Lincoln I knew where Lisa lived, noticing Chuck not contributing a bit. Chuck and I piled in the squad car and the three of us started for her place.

Her apartment building had looked better at night. In the light of day I could see that the ferns of the fern bar on the first floor (closed till two P.M.) were plastic. The outside of the building needed paint on the trim and the stairwell leading up to her place smelled like urine. I guess I was just too damn horny to notice that before. We knocked on the door and after about a minute we heard movement and a sleepy voice asking who it was.

"Lisa? It's me. Milt. Gotta talk to you."

She opened the door with a smile on her face, which faded when she saw the other two men with me.

With one hand on one lovely hip, she said, "Little early in the day for something this kinky, don't ja think, Milt?"

Lincoln showed her his shield and she backed away, allowing us inside. "Mind if I use your phone a minute, ma'am?"

She showed him where it was and he called the dispatcher, leaving Lisa's number so they could call back with the information on Al Taylor.

After he got off the phone, I said, "Why don't you just ask her? She'll probably know."

He nodded. "Ma'am, you happen to have the address on Al Taylor?"

Lisa sat down on the couch. Her color wasn't so good. "Yeah. I know where he lives. Why do you want to know?"

"We have reason to belive that Mr. Taylor took a shot at Mr. Kovak here and Mr. Lancaster. This morning."

Lisa's color went from bad to real bad. "Daddy?" she asked.

Chuck and I looked at each other and both mouthed "Daddy?" while Lincoln got down to business.

"Al Taylor's your father, ma'am?"

"I wanna lawyer," was all Al's little girl would say.

THIRTEEN

I HADN'T TOLD anybody much what had been going on. We were waiting for Lincoln to do that. Me, Chuck, Jewel, and Honey. Chuck was sweating bullets and I can't say I felt that sorry for him, or envied him much either. He just kept say, "Honey, baby, this wasn't my fault..." and Honey kept saying, "What isn't your fault?" and Chuck would just shake his head and I'd just say, "Wait till Lincoln gets here." Which is what we did.

Finally, around three in the afternoon, Lincoln showed up. He said hidy to everybody, pulled up a chair, and sat down. "Sorry it took so long, but once we got that guy to talkin' we could hardly shut him up."

"You found the man who murdered Henry?" Jewel asked, struggling to sit up in bed.

"Not the man who actually pulled the trigger, but the one who hired him, we did."

"Why?" Jewel said. "Why?"

And that's when great, big old foul-mouthed Chuck fell to his knees beside my sister's bed and burst into tears. "It's all my fault!" he wailed. "All my fault!"

Lincoln and I got him upright again and sitting in a chair where he proceeded to try to sniffle his way out of the trouble he'd soon be in with his wife. And Lincoln started to explain.

First he explained to Jewel who Al was and what he did for a living. "Anyway, Al's got this daughter, Lisa, been living with his ex-wife in Dallas since they got a divorce when the girl was about fifteen. So this girl, Lisa, comes to live with her daddy when she drops out of college about six months ago. Well, far as Al's concerned, this is his baby girl, the same sweet little thing he left at the age of fifteen. Of course, according to the girl's mama, she'd gotten herself kicked out of Baylor on a morals charge in the first place. Something to do with a married professor. Anyway, Al sees this married man at his bar sniffin' around his baby girl..."

"Henry?" Jewel asked, her eyes closed against the inevitable.

Here Lincoln started to hem and haw a bit and finally said, "Well, no ma'am." He looked at Honey and said, "Miz Lancaster, I hate to be the one to say this, but the man Al was trying to kill was your husband here." Now Lincoln wasn't looking at Honey, and neither was anybody else in the room. Poor Chuck had his eyes glued to his size thirteens, and I personally had me a real good view of the light fixture.

"Chuck?" Honey said softly. "Chuck!" Not so softly. "Look at me!"

Chuck lifted his head and stared somewhat in his wife's direction. "What did you do?"

"Baby..."

"What did you do?"

"Sweetheart..."

Unfortunately there was a Houston telephone book sitting on Jewel's bedside table. Honey picked it up, stood up, walked over to Chuck, and wammed him upside the head with it. And let me tell you, Houston phone books are big.

The gist of the whole thing was that Al Taylor liked to sample his product a bit too much, and got juiced on a regular basis. One night he saw his darlin' Lisa join Chuck outside the bar after hours. Al was drunker than he oughta been and he got the Mexican man who swept up the bar after hours to drive so they could follow Chuck and Al's baby girl. Him and the Mexican sat outside Lisa's apartment drinking from the bottle Al had brought along till they saw Chuck leave in the wee hours. By that time the Mexican was too drunk to drive so Al took over and followed Chuck home.

All the way to Chuck's house Al and the Mexican, who Al claimed was named Rafael Guzman, discussed how this wasn't right and how a father had his honor to uphold and on and on. So, after two days of more hardcore drinking and philosophizing, Al and Guzman came up with a plan. For five hundred dollars Guzman would kill Chuck, save Lisa's virtue, and bring honor back to Al. Al figured it was a hell of a bargain. Naturally, Al and Rafael had had a few drinks to seal the bargain, so that when Guzman left to do his duty, he got lost and ended up at the wrong house—and shot the wrong man. According to Al, shooting Jewel hadn't been part of the deal. He called it "improvising" on Rafael's part.

When Guzman shot the wrong man, Al got pissed and called immigration. As far as he knew, Rafael was now down somewhere in Mexico.

That's when I came into the picture. Al heard Lisa making a date with me on the phone and tried hiring his dirty work out again. This time to the nephews of a Vietnamese bar owner down the street from After Hours. They're the ones who beat me up, but Lincoln said he'd have a hard time proving it. Their wives, mothers, and four aunts all vouched for their whereabouts at the time I was getting the dog piss beat outta me. I got to thinking that the whole thing coulda been sorta funny, if it hadn't been for the fact that Henry was dead and Jewel was hurt.

The wiring of the stove in Jewel's house and the wiring of Chuck's car had both been done by Al himself. He just got plum tired of hiring out and he said he was running short of funds anyway. He learned the little trick with the stove during the Korean War, working for Uncle himself. He tried to blow me up because he saw me leaving Lisa's apartment. He tried again with the Porsche not to get me or Honey, but because the night before, after I'd found out Lisa's age and decided maybe I'd better act mine, Chuck himself had come a-courting.

You know that song, "If It Weren't for Bad Luck I'd Have No Luck at All"? Well, I figured old Al should have that carved into his headstone when the time comes, and the time won't come too soon for me.

After Lincoln finished his tale, we all sat there quietly, with only Chuck's occasional moan to interrupt the silence. Finally Lincoln said, "Well, I got reports to write so I'd best be on my way." Turning to Jewel, he said, "Miz Hotchkiss, I'm sorry things turned out the way they did. But I'm just glad I'm not arresting you for anything."

"There's always that," Jewel said quietly.

Lincoln left. Jewel and I looked at each other. Finally, she said, "Milton, why don't you roll me down to the solarium in this wheelchair?" Which is what I did as quickly as possible, leaving Chuck and Honey alone together. Probably, as a peace officer, I should have stayed. But I figured whatever Honey did to him, Chuck deserved.

When we got back to the room, they were gone. The only sign of them having been there were the spilled flowers and broken vase near the chair Chuck had occupied.

Three days later, Honey and I were in the hospital elevator with our hands full. Me with two ivy plants and her with a pot of mums and a vase of carnations. Three more potted plants rode in Jewel Anne's lap while the nurse pushed the wheelchair.

"I can walk," Jewel Anne said for the forty-second time as we waited for the elevator.

"Hospital rules, Mrs. Hotchkiss." Jewel Anne just sighed.

I figured I'd be hearing a lot of that over the next few years. What with Jewel Anne and the kids moving back to Prophesy County with me. Jewel and I had talked about that the night before. Right after she'd talked a lot about Henry.

"He was a good man, Milt," she'd said.

I'd just nodded my head. "I know you've found out things you didn't want to know. I found out some things, too. I never knew about the other women. I suspected from time to time that he might be having a fling, but I guess I just didn't want to know." Again, I just nodded my head. "He loved me a lot."

"I know that for a fact."

"And I loved him."

I didn't even raise an eyebrow. Sometimes I have so much control it's scary.

"We were married for sixteen years, Milton. You can't stay married that long if there isn't love there."

Again I just nodded my head and brought up her and the kids moving back home with me.

"My home's here," she'd said.

"Well, I know that. But what's keeping you here really? I got this great big house and a corral where we could put some horses. How many friends you got here, besides Honey?"

"Milton..."

"Last time I talked to Glenda Sue, she said she'd been getting calls from all sorts of people back home. Mavis Pettigrew? Remember her? Mavis Davis now since she married Bert. Glenda Sue said she's been calling almost every day threatening to come down to Houston and shove something up somebody's ass so's they'd listen."

Jewel Anne laughed. "That sounds like Mavis! God, I haven't seen or heard from her since high school!"

"And Harmon Monk? Glenda Sue said he'd called more 'n' once a day."

Jewel Anne blushed. "I wouldn't know why," she said.

"And the Haverston twins. Eloise and Isabelle? They started a defense collection. Last I heard they had a hundred and twenty-seven dollars."

My little sister laughed and then got quiet for a minute. "God, I had no idea."

"Lot of people in Longbranch love you a lot, little girl. Including me."

I didn't look at her when I said that and I figured she probably wasn't looking at me either. Being the first time I ever even got close to saying "I love you" to my sister, it was kinda rough on both of us.

I coughed a couple of times then said, "The master bedroom's on the first floor. You can have that. Doc says you'll be having some trouble with stairs. There's two bedrooms upstairs that Marlene and Carl can have and an extra room up there I can turn into my bedroom."

"What about Leonard?"

I grinned. "Well, there's this apartment over the garage. Big ole place. Give the boy a little freedom and a little incentive for moving to hicksville. And we got real live psychiatrist moved to Longbranch about a year ago. Leonard's doing so well with the social worker here, he could just continue that up there for a while."

She shook her head. "God, Milton, I don't know..."

"There's a room off the living room, kinda a sun room, I guess you'd call it. Your baby grand'd fit in there real nice."

It's funny sometimes what a decision can be based on. All the love coming her way from all the people of her old hometown, including her old high school boyfriend, the grand country life up to and including horses, plenty of room for her kids to spread out, a brother as wonderful as me, and what finally decided her was her baby grand having a room of its own.

The kids had just gotten back from school when we pulled in the driveway. Jewel Anne burst into tears when she saw the sign covering the front of the house, made out of about twenty-seven sheets of Chuck's computer paper, saying *WELCOME HOME, JEWEL*!!!

My cheeks still stung from blowing up all the balloons we had taped to every available surface of the living room and den. Jewel laughed and cried and hugged everybody, except me.

She was still leaning kinda heavy on the cane I'd bought her at a medical supply house. Dr. Hussain said she'd probably use it the rest of her life. There was nothing wrong with her leg, but the part of her brain that told her left leg to move wasn't much there anymore.

So we had a party. Me and my baby sister and her kids and Chuck and Honey and two of the ladies who'd supplied the food while we'd been living in Jewel's house. She was a little disappointed to see the boarded-up windows and the destruction of her kitchen, but I guess the thought of her baby grand with a room of its own took some of the sting out of the mess.

Marlene took the fact that she'd been right, that the killer just had the wrong damn house, as a given. She didn't need any explanation. Honey, on the other hand, wasn't speaking to Chuck and had been flirting with me in front of everybody like a son of a bitch. But she didn't shoot him, she didn't cut off his balls, or anything else.

A week after Jewel Anne got out of the hospital, we had her car packed to the brim with kids and plants and the furniture loaded up by Allied. Chuck had said his good-byes as he'd left for work, but Honey was standing by the car bawling.

She and Jewel Anne held on to each other for about a month, then without a word, Jewel kissed her on the mouth, sobbed, and got into the car. I walked over and put my hand on Honey's head. "You okay?" I asked.

"Yeah. Shit. I'm gonna miss them."

"I know."

She looked up at me and laughed, sorta. "Gonna miss you too."

I sighed. "Stop flirting with me, woman. I'm only human."

"It woulda been great."

"Who you been talking to?"

She giggled. "Don't think you'd get a good recommendation?"

"I gotta go."

"I know."

"What's gonna happen? Between you and Chuck?"

She sighed. "I dunno. If you'd asked me a month ago what I'd do if I found out he'd been cheating on me, I would've told you I'd kill him. Or, at the very least castrate him. But now..." She shrugged her pretty little shoulders. "I figure I'll just make his life miserable for a couple of years. And if he's a good boy, then maybe I'll forgive him." She looked off at the house then back at me. "His mother's given us the name of a marriage counselor. Seemed she and Daddy Paul went through the same thing." She shrugged.

"Think he'll go?" I asked.

She pulled herself up to her full five feet. "You bet your sweet ass he'll go."

I grinned. "Yes, ma'am."

She reached up and kissed the side of my mouth. "But I still say what's good for the goose..."

I walked around to the driver's side of the car. "If you're ever in Oklahoma without the hulk..."

She smiled and I got in and drove north, seeing in the rearview mirror not Houston, but a hell of a lady named Honey.

MURDER
WITHOUT RESERVATION

A TONY AND PAT PRATT MYSTERY

BERNIE LEE

With only three more major sequences left to shoot, the picture looked like a successful wrap. But that was before somebody shot the horse and the drug dealer, before Tony went crashing through white-water rapids to save a terrified boy from drowning, before the runaway grass fire and way before somebody dumped a pair of deadly rattlesnakes in the Pratts' bedroom....

POISON PEN

A CHARLOTTE KENT MYSTERY

MARY KITTREDGE

A DEB RALSTON MYSTERY

DEFICIT ENDING
LEE MARTIN

Ready or not, Ralston is back from maternity leave, haunted by the look of a young teller who is taken hostage and later killed— the first in a string of victims.

Deb Ralston is soon hot on the tail of the murderers and heading straight into deadly danger.